Forever and Ever Always

by

Sue C. Dugan

The Soul Exchange Trilogy

Cover Art by *Tina Lynn Stout*

The Wild Rose Press, Inc.
PO Box 708
Adams Basin, NY 14410-0708
Visit us at www.thewildrosepress.com

Publishing History
First Edition, 2025
Trade Paperback ISBN 978-1-5092-6086-7
Digital ISBN 978-1-5092-6087-4

The Soul Exchange Trilogy
Published in the United States of America

Dedication

Forever and Ever, Always is dedicated to my wonderful family for their love and support during the writing, editing, and publishing process. This book is also dedicated to Amy Tipton (Feral Girl Books) who has reviewed all my books and helped me craft them into what they are today.

Prologue

Sabrina found herself in a bright place after the accident. With her body shrouded in mist, her feet moved on their own. She moved toward an even brighter glow.

When she got closer, she saw a woman standing at the end. Was she an angel? She looked sort of like an angel without wings—her hair floated around her head in a golden halo.

"Hello," Sabrina said, timidly looking around. "Who are you?"

"I'm Alison."

"Alison?"

"I was in an accident."

Sabrina paused. "I think I caused that accident."

Alison stood there, her hands clasped. "We have to decide."

"Decide what?" Sabrina asked. She shrugged. "What's to decide?"

"My soul wants to live," Alison explained, "but my body has died. We can switch bodies."

"Is that a thing?" Sabrina asked.

"It is if you don't want to be here," Alison answered.

Sabrina shuddered as she felt them administering to her broken body. If she looked down, she saw the lights of the ambulance highlight someone on a gurney.

Her? They were jolting her alive.

Did she want to be here? She didn't like living in Clearwater, Michigan. She had no friends, her parents weren't well, and she had no hope for the future. What the heck. "Yes, I'll switch with you. What do I do?"

"Nothing," Alison said. "They'll save your body and my soul will live with you."

"What about me—my soul?" Sabrina shuddered again. "They're trying to revive me."

"Let them," Alison said. "Your soul will leave. I promise, it will just walk away."

And with that, Sabrina's soul walked away and Alison's soul took over. Alison's soul was now in Sabrina's body; for all intents and purposes, Alison became Sabrina. Alison would have dual memories now, too.

Alison watched Sabrina leave and slipped inside the girl's body. Sabrina turned when from far below, she heard, "We have a heartbeat!"

Chapter 1

Prison was depressing—four gray walls, bars, and limited freedom or privacy. Sabrina Timmons had a choice—accept the consequences of her actions or wallow in self-pity or depression.

She pulled on her big girl panties and slowly acclimated herself to life behind bars and used the time to work on her GED and read as many books as she could cram in from the small library. Some of the books were dog-eared and water-stained like someone had spilled something or cried into the pages.

She could understand the crying part. She had spent the first few days here bawling her eyes out while some of the other women circled her hungrily—a lamb to slaughter.

"So you don't think you should be here?" another prisoner had cackled.

"Honey, none of us should be here." A tall, heavyset woman stroked Sabrina's hair while smirking. "But you don't see us crying and blubbering, do you?"

Sabrina squeezed her eyes shut, hoping and praying when she opened them she'd be back in high school. But that didn't happen. She had hated high school, but she had changed.

She had been tried as an adult even though she was seventeen. She seemed to be the youngest woman in here.

So when she dried her tears and looked around, she was still in prison with other women who said they hadn't done what they were accused of either. But she meant it. She had watched someone else drive her car into a moving van, tumbling it over the guardrail, its contents littering the hill—a broken baby crib, pots and pans, and a tangle of clothing. The one thing she remembered vividly was the broken and battered baby crib, like Lincoln logs—pulled apart and scattered about.

The woman in the van was having a baby, and now that baby had no mother or crib.

"I don't remember doing that terrible thing," Sabrina had lamented during counseling.

The other women folded their arms and nodded knowingly. "I was framed, too."

"It was like someone else drove my car," Sabrina said.

"And the devil made me kill my ex," a woman said with a snort.

Sabrina didn't think it was the devil. Her court records and attorney told her she was high. The chemicals sizzled in her veins, making her unhappiness disappear until they caused more unhappiness than they masked. What had the chemicals in the drugs done to her body, to her mind?

Sabrina got no sympathy so she decided to get on with her sentence and make the most of it. She received five years because the husband of the woman she had killed asked for leniency. His name was Henry Comstock. She read about him and his wife in the newspaper. Five years—sixty months—one thousand, eight hundred and twenty-five days for taking someone's life.

Now she had served five months and had fifty-five more to go.

She thought of that man, Henry Comstock, many times. She felt an invisible tug toward him. That was curious. She had only seen him in court a couple of times and they hadn't spoken directly to each other, but still she felt she had known him. Maybe it was just someone like him?

In court, she had covertly watched Henry with a baby. The baby was wrapped in a tight pink cocoon and was quiet—a girl. For some reason, Sabrina couldn't keep her eyes off the baby and her stomach hurt from a longing she had never experienced before.

She didn't have a stomachache like she'd eaten something sour. No, it was more of a longing that brought tears to her eyes or a part of her heart had ripped away. She didn't have a very good view of Henry or the baby; even if she sat up straighter and craned her neck, she only saw the pink blanket. Her fingers moved restlessly as if they were stroking the soft blanket that cradled the baby's face. Her attorney frowned at her fidgeting, but didn't stop her.

Henry looked and felt familiar although she didn't know why. Of course, his picture was in the paper too, but it was something deeper and more intrinsic. Lately, her thoughts had been scrambled, as if her brain had been put in a blender.

Perhaps, that's what the drugs had done to her— made her thoughts unrecognizable and foreign until she didn't know who she was.

She thought about Henry and his kid when she couldn't sleep on her small, cramped cot and thin blanket. His eyes. Yes, she concentrated on his liquid brown eyes—the color of coffee with no cream. And the baby, she had blue eyes—wide with wonder and the joy of living. Yes, she felt comforted when she thought of Henry and his baby.

Chapter 2

The loudspeaker squawked and spewed forth the daily announcements. Sabrina sighed. Prison had been good for keeping her on a schedule. She gathered her books for class—she was almost finished with her GED.

For some reason, school made more sense now, and she passed several classes just by testing out of them. *Did I know I could write like that?* She shrugged and decided not to worry about how or why she had passed writing composition—she just did.

Now, Sabrina went into the makeshift classroom with tables and chairs, got her work, and nodded to the officer who supervised the class. At this rate, she would probably finish before her sentence was up—forty-eight months to go.

"What are you working on today, Sabrina?" the teacher asked. Officer Lawrence sat in the back of the classroom and observed.

"English."

Although Sabrina hadn't liked English before, now it was her favorite subject. And her reading had improved one hundred percent. It was amazing how her point of view had shifted. Was it her age? She was now eighteen. Had she always been this way and didn't realize it? Or could it be all the books she had checked out of the library?

"What book are you reading?" the teacher asked.

"*Little Women.*"

There had been a list of classics to choose from: *Moby Dick*, *The Grapes of Wrath*, etc. But she thought *Little Women* sounded better than whales or grapes. In the deep recesses of her mind, she remembered reading those books—she just couldn't remember when.

"A favorite!" the teacher said before dipping her chin to acknowledge another inmate who entered the room. "You'll need to write a book report on that." She tapped the cover before moving on.

"I will," Sabrina promised and opened it to where she had left off—chapter twenty-three. Sabrina slouched down in the unyielding plastic chair—orange, like their unflattering jumpsuits, and began reading, but her mind went in another direction. She questioned her memory of reading this book before, but for the life of her, she couldn't pinpoint when. It must have been in school. She had read all the suggested books at one time or another.

A memory/thought flashed through her mind. She stood at the front of a class, reading this very book and asking the classroom, "What are the characters' motivations?"

How could that thought be possible though? Sure, she wanted to be a teacher. Wait, she did? That was news to her…wasn't it?

Sabrina pushed aside the dream and went back to reading.

The March family's motivations were similar to Sabrina's. Although this story took place during the Civil War—a far different time and place. But it was interesting how they made the best of their situation.

Sort of like now, Sabrina mused. She was in prison and had time to kill.

That was perhaps a poor way to think of it—time to kill...*time to spare,* she reworded her thought. She had time to read and think and ponder the unfairness of life.

The counselor told her jail sobered a person. She was sober, for sure.

The March family was poor, and Sabrina could also relate to that. Her parents were working poor—holding menial jobs that barely covered rent and food. Sabrina frowned at the memory of stealing clothing from a local store.

In her mind's eye, she clearly remembered going into the dressing room and wearing two or three blouses out of the store—but the memory seemed to be of someone else. Maybe one of her friends had done that?

Oh, how Sabrina wished she could go back to before the accident that killed Alison Larkin-Comstock. Sabrina knew about Alison from the newspaper. Alison was a teacher, and she, Henry, and their baby had been driving toward a new life in Indiana when Sabrina caused the accident.

She fantasized about Henry and his baby.

Did all people think about the victims of their crimes? She wanted to rub her cheeks along the soft hair on the top of the baby's head—the delicate, silk-like strands tickling her nose. It was pure torture to continue to think about them, but she couldn't help it. Should she ask the priest who came weekly? Was this normal?

She blew out her breath and pushed aside that thought. She wouldn't finish the book if she continued to daydream and tried to concentrate on the story before her. But Henry intruded again. How did she know they were going to Indiana exactly? Had the newspaper said that? She didn't think so and frowned at the memory of walking around a university.

She was sure it was a college. There were signs for different buildings—College of Science, College of Medicine—a library, and students with bicycles and backpacks. Yes, Henry was going to college. She knew this. Somehow she knew it. He wanted to be a doctor. Her actions had robbed him of his dreams, too.

She blew out her breath and concentrated on the March sisters: Amy, Jo, Beth, and Meg.

****

Later that week, Sabrina helped in the kitchen. She had learned to follow a recipe and cook. This evening, though, she was helping serve hamburgers and potatoes. Her mind wandered again as she watched the familiar women file past with their trays. None of them were terrible and she could easily sympathize with them—Sabrina knew she wasn't a bad person either.

She had been mad at her parents for making her move to Clearwater—an impossible distance from Detroit. She had been in trouble before they moved, but for different reasons. In Clearwater, she hung with the troublemakers hiding behind the green dumpsters in the back of the school. That's where she met Danny. Together, they dodged the janitors by crouching down, smoking, taking pills, and watching some of the girls carve up their arms.

She had scars, too, from when her body had been projected through the windshield.

"I said no potatoes!"

The angry voice jerked Sabrina away from her thoughts. She closed her eyes, remembered Henry and the baby, blew out her breath, before opening her eyes with a smile plastered on her face. "Sorry," she said. "I guess I didn't hear you." She smiled again at the woman, whose face softened a bit as she went to the next food station.

"I want extra fruit!" the woman demanded.

Someone must be having a bad day. Sabrina rolled her eyes. She understood though—it was easy to have a bad day here.

While in prison, Sabrina had a chance to think through what made her take drugs and why she was in such a rage over her parents' cross-state move. The move was out of Sabrina's control. Drugs made her forget her pain and troubles. Not the best way to handle the situation, she had decided after going to counseling and examining why she was in prison. When she got out, she swore she'd concentrate on paying her restitution to Henry Comstock and his daughter. That is, *if* she could get a job.

Being a felon limited her choices. She had wanted to be a teacher, but that was out of the question now. Now, she might have to settle for work in a warehouse.

She had talked to the prison chaplain, who came once a week to counsel the women about their feelings, healing through prayer, and asking for forgiveness. He was a kindly man named Christopher who listened patiently as she explained she had killed someone.

Father Christopher was young and didn't look the way she had thought ministers or priests were supposed to look. But then again, did she look like someone capable of manslaughter?

After Father Christopher asked how she was doing, Sabrina launched into what was on her mind.

"The thing is…" Sabrina chewed on her lip. "Why don't I remember killing Alison Comstock?"

"Your body blocked it?" Father Christopher suggested and shrugged. He wore a cross around his neck that swayed as he talked. He seemed to be always moving or twitching. Sabrina could tell he didn't like to sit still.

"But I keep thinking about them," she said. Watching his cross was hypnotizing.

He frowned. "Who?"

"Henry Comstock and his baby daughter." She moved her gaze from his cross to his face.

Father Christopher was looking at her with narrowed, confused eyes, but remained quiet as if waiting for her to continue.

"Is this how God is punishing me?" When she was stressed, she closed her eyes and pictured Henry and his kid.

"My child, he doesn't do things like that."

Sabrina shook her head. She still didn't understand.

The next week when Father Christopher came, she was still hypnotized by his cross pendant, saying the first things that came to mind, like being on autopilot. In fact, she said, "I feel as if I've become a different person."

He chuckled. "I hear that a lot. When you're free of drugs, your mind has a chance to function properly." He shifted in his seat.

She scowled and chewed on her bottom lip some more. "This may sound woo-woo, but do souls grow back in a body? Another body?"

He raised his brows as if he was considering her words. The cross rested squarely on his chest and didn't move.

"I think I damaged my soul in the accident," Sabrina's tongue felt thick but she kept talking, "and might have a new one."

"Like a change of heart?" His fingers fluttered toward his necklace.

"Maybe." She scratched her chin, remembering a bright place after the accident where she got a new soul. It was hard to describe, the details were fuzzy, and the parameters moved. Had it been a dream? It felt like a dream.

"There are many stories in the Bible about people who have found Christ and changed their lives."

She slowly shook her head. *My situation wasn't like that.*

"Is there anything in the Bible about soul switching?" She stabbed at her Bible with her finger as if forcing her words into it.

He raised his eyebrows. "Not that I know of."

"That's what I thought." Sabrina slumped in her seat. "I've been searching for soul switching in the Bible but can't find anything."

"Why do you think you have a new soul?" he asked, leaning forward expectantly.

"Isn't the soul the essence of a person?" Her gaze held on his cross necklace, dangling with his forward-leaning posture.

"I believe so."

"I'm a completely different person and have memories that seem foreign and strange, yet I remember them. It's like there are two people in my body."

"A good one and a bad one?"

"Sort of."

"Ah!" He smiled knowingly. "Have you asked for forgiveness?"

She felt her eyes fill with tears that itched and stung. "I have! Yes, daily!" She grabbed a tissue from the box, blew her nose, and wiped her tears against her hand.

Closing her eyes, she pictured Henry and his baby and felt a calm descend over her body. She opened her eyes still surrounded by the peaceful feeling she got when she pictured the baby with Henry.

When she calmed, he said, "That's a start."

"Can you tell me why I feel this way?"

"No, only you can discover the answer through your prayers and the grace of God."

"I've been praying every day." She sniffed.

"Prayers may hold the answers if you're supposed to know them."

"Am I supposed to know?" she asked.

"Possibly." Father Christopher's fingers drummed on his Bible.

"Henry Comstock, the man whose wife I killed, has a baby." She sniffled and reached for another tissue. "That poor kid won't have a mother because of me. He has forgiven me for her death, but..." Sabrina shook her head.

Father Christopher just nodded. "But have you forgiven yourself?"

"I think...maybe?" She wasn't sure. Had she forgiven herself for the accident? Could she? "No." Sabrina looked up. "I don't think I have."

"That may be the first step toward redemption."

Sabrina nodded—forgiveness was easier said than done.

They sat and looked at each other. Father Christopher leaned forward waiting for her to speak.

She blew out a long breath and said, "When I get out, after I've paid my restitution, I want to go to college and earn a degree to help others."

"Have you always wanted to do that?"

"No," she said with a sigh. "The accident changed me, though, remember? I don't feel like myself anymore."

He coughed. "Prison has a way of doing that to a person."

She shrugged one shoulder. This was her first time in prison, and she vowed it would be the last.

He patted her hand. "How much longer?"

She thought back. "Forty-eight months."

"It'll go by fast."

It hadn't so far.

Chapter 3

Father Christopher was right—forty months flew by. Sabrina had been almost too busy to notice the months slip away while she read, studied, and discovered the "new" person she had become.

"Congratulations to the following students who finished their GED courses: Sabrina Timmons, Rhonda Bolenski, Chennin Zeno…" the loudspeaker crackled out the names.

When her parents visited, Sabrina showed them her GED certificate.

"I finished!" She excitedly jerked it up and down.

Sabrina's mother gave her a small smile. "Congratulations." And then looked away, as if she was embarrassed.

Sabrina knew neither of her parents had graduated from high school, but she had. Couldn't they be happy for her?

"That's nice," her father said. "Will it help you get a job?"

"I hope so." She placed the certificate on the table in front of her and smoothed out the crumpled edges from holding it.

"Then, it's good," he said.

They left, and when she met with Father Christopher, she brought along her certificate.

"Look!" She held up the piece of paper. "I finished

high school!"

His smile was warm and genuine. "That's quite an accomplishment!"

She shrugged and tried to act like it was nothing, but it wasn't nothing. She was on a roll with education and had signed up for community college classes offered through the prison.

"It will look good on your record when you come before the review board."

That was a year or so away.

"What are you planning to study?" Father Christopher asked.

"I wanted to major in child development and early education, but the counselor here said I should do something with business." Her mouth turned down as she thought about her conversation with the counselor.

"Education?" the counselor with '80's hair, teased and puffed up, had said. She came to the prison once a month to speak to the women. "You won't be able to work with children with a prison record." She shook her head and frowned. Then, her face brightened. "Your best bet would be a job in an office or a store or warehouse."

"I had my heart set on being a teacher."

"That won't happen," the counselor repeated. "Think about something else. Even general studies is good."

Sabrina blew out a breath, closed her eyes envisioning Henry's baby in the pink blanket, smelling sweetly of talcum powder and lotion, and she felt calmer and said, "General studies, it is."

A student raised their hand and said, "A little help over here! I don't get these math problems."

Sabrina gritted her teeth but kept a smile plastered to her face. If she couldn't be a legitimate teacher, maybe she could tutor other woman prisoners during GED classes.

The next week, she showed up in the GED classroom. The teacher had raised her brows when Sabrina entered the room.

"Sabrina! And what do I owe this pleasure?"

"Can I help tutor the women in reading and English?" Sabrina asked.

The teacher raised her brows again. "I don't see why not. You're finished, and you're quite good at English and reading."

"Thank you!" Sabrina beamed.

Her first student was Audrey, a woman in her mid-40s who was missing a front tooth. Audrey continued to probe the empty spot with her tongue, further drawing attention to it.

"I'm here to help with English if you need it." Sabrina sat quietly and folded her hands.

Audrey studied her. "You're pretty young."

"Twenty." Sabrina nodded. "And I finished my GED."

Audrey raised her brows, then said, "Sure, you can help me. I don't like to read. I'm not very good. The words seem to move around the page, and I forget what they said."

"You might have dyslexia," Sabrina said before she thought about her response.

Audrey studied Sabrina with her head tilted to one side. "What?" she asked. "What's that?"

"You have trouble sounding out words and reading with fluency," Sabrina said matter-of-factly and gasped.

How exactly did she know what dyslexia was? Another puzzling piece of information from her brain.

"Can you help me?"

"Yes." Again, Sabrina surprised herself. "We'll practice reading every day."

With a wrinkled nose and a skeptical look, Audrey agreed.

****

Sabrina worked with Audrey until she could almost read a page without continuous help. Yes, Sabrina smiled; she liked being a teacher. She was good at it. Too bad, she couldn't be one when she got out of prison.

Had Henry Comstock been able to go to college? She hoped he had become a doctor. He was ambitious.

Wait. How did she know that? *He seemed ambitious*, she silently corrected herself.

Again, she had those thoughts that were familiar, yet unfamiliar. *I feel like I know him...but you don't*, she reminded herself. *You don't.*

Chapter 4

Sabrina met with the parole board after serving forty-eight months. She was twenty-two years old and a completely different person than when she first arrived.

The hearing was in a long, narrow room with a big wooden table for the board members. She couldn't see their names clearly, but her attorney told her one was a judge, another from the governor's office, and another a psychiatrist.

Other prisoners were sitting in the audience with people who looked like attorneys—their suits, ties, heels, and briefcases giving them away in a sea of orange jumpsuits.

Sabrina sat next to her attorney, Logan. She glanced around the room until she saw Henry Comstock. He had aged since her original trial.

He was still tall with a chiseled face and compassionate gaze, but his face now had a few lines around his brown eyes, and his blondish-brown hair was cut short. His forehead scar showed but was faint and almost indistinguishable from the rest of his face.

She had a matching scar on her cheek and reached up to touch the raised line. Did Henry ever touch his scar, too? She was disappointed he hadn't brought his daughter. Sabrina wanted to see her.

Sabrina knew she should turn around and face the panel, but she couldn't help herself. Henry gave her a brief nod before Logan tapped on her arm to turn around.

"Sabrina Timmons," the judge announced.

Logan led her to a table in front of the panel.

"We've been reviewing your prison record and find your actions evidence of your rehabilitation. We believe you may be able to function as a productive citizen in the general population again. You've received your GED and associate degree in science and have tutored other prisoners," he read.

Sabrina looked around and saw several heads nod, and a couple of the women she had helped gave her a thumbs-up. Her heart was hammering so loud she thought it might break through her chest. Did this mean…was she…free?

Sabrina saw the judge look beyond her. She turned when Henry stood up. Henry straightened his shirt and cleared his throat. "Your honor," he began. He looked so nervous Sabrina wanted to give him a hug. "I support the decision to release Sabrina Timmons from prison. I feel she made a grievous mistake at seventeen and has proven she can be a responsible and contributing member of society." He gave a small smile before saying thank you and sitting down.

Oh, Henry, Sabrina thought, *thank you! I promise it was a mistake, a big—huge—mistake. I won't make it again. I'll spend the rest of my life contributing to society. You'll see.*

The judge nodded firmly. "Thank you, for your comments, Doctor Comstock."

Doctor Comstock! Sabrina released a small smile. He had finished medical school! At least she hadn't upended his college plans, too.

Emotion swirled around her, and she sniffed. Logan must have sensed she was tearing up because he pushed the tissue box toward her.

"The verdict?" The judge looked over at the other members on the board.

One person stood, sliding a folder down the table. "We find you eligible to return to society," they pronounced.

They continued speaking about what she would need to do on parole, but she tuned them out. *Free!* She'd be able to come and go as she pleased. Her mind jumped from one possibility to another.

"We, therefore, remand you to the parole board, where you must complete the requirements of your sentence."

She must pay restitution and couldn't drive a car until she was twenty-three—which wasn't far off.

She was free! She pinched her arm to make sure she wasn't dreaming.

As Sabrina walked out with Logan, they passed Henry. The men nodded to each other. Logan stuck out his hand, and Henry shook it.

"How are you doing?" Logan asked.

"Good, thanks for asking."

Did Henry know Logan? She stood there awkwardly, tuning out their small talk, until a thought popped into her mind. Another of those thoughts that were hers, but not. The confusion caused by head trauma.

She remembered that Logan had been Henry's lawyer during...during what? Did she know? Had Logan told her? The thought confused her. The men stopped and looked at her when she sniffed and raised her sleeve to wipe her eyes, and she gave Henry a watery smile as tears threatened to overwhelm her.

She couldn't believe she would be free soon and he had spoken up for her. After what she had done, it was hard to believe he had forgiven her. He showed her a small smile and a dip of his chin before reaching into his pocket and pulling out a tissue. She mouthed "thank you" to him.

"No problem." Henry dismissed her thanks with a quick wave. "I have a child so I always need tissues."

She gave a short laugh, and they continued to stare at each other until Logan nudged her elbow. Henry opened his mouth at one point to say something but then closed it as if he thought better of it. Logan left her at the prison, and now she waited for the paperwork to be processed for her departure.

It seemed to take days until she was released. *Couldn't they hurry?* She wanted to get out of here. She absently gnawed at a hangnail as her mind screamed—hurry, hurry, hurry!

When the day of her release finally came (it took two weeks actually), an officer brought in a brown paper bag with her clothes. The clothes she had worn when she was imprisoned. Sabrina dumped out the bag and studied the ripped jeans, a tiny tee shirt that wouldn't cover much of anything, and a sweatshirt with gaping holes. After wearing a prison uniform for almost five years, these felt foreign to her. But with nothing else to wear, she shuffled into the nearest bathroom and tugged them on.

Turning to study her reflection in the mirror, she smoothed out her top and patted down her jeans. They still fit, but she couldn't imagine wearing them to work or anywhere else. In fact, she grimaced at her reflection. She wouldn't be caught dead in a get-up like this now.

She blew out her breath, making her bangs flutter on her forehead. Just as she was pushing her bangs aside, there was pounding on the door.

"You ready?" the guard asked.

"Yes." Sabrina threw open the door.

Her parents were waiting to take her home in their battered blue Honda. Before getting in, she pumped an arm to the sky. *Thank you, Jesus, for letting me out!* Then she settled into her parents' car for the ride to their apartment, watching the sights go by. She missed seeing trees and children playing, or even the sound of dogs barking.

After getting settled, she decided the first thing would be getting new clothing, clothing that covered her body—nothing tight-fitting or ripped. She'd need to find a job and wanted to look like she was responsible enough to get to and from work. She didn't think the clothing she wore in high school fit the image she wanted to project now.

Chapter 5

Home was another apartment she had never been in before, yet it looked like all the others. Her parents hopscotched from one low-income place to another, oftentimes skipping out on the rent because they chose to buy drugs or alcohol with the money. Sabrina didn't recognize this apartment, but they were all similar: bare-bones, cheap tile, threadbare carpeting, blinds that hung askew, walls of nondescript light-beige paint— bland as the rice pudding they used to serve in the prison cafeteria. Smoke hung heavy in the still air. Sabrina's nose twitched, and she felt the urge to sneeze.

Since this was a one-bedroom, Sabrina was relegated to the lumpy couch. Her things from before her incarceration were stored in a box in the storage closet. Just one measly box. She stared at it, blinking.

Her mother answered her unspoken question, "We had to get rid of most of your things when we moved."

Figured.

She had fantasized about a different home—not this depressing one. Was it wishful thinking she'd be released to a home with a comfy chair for reading and a lamp that glowed yellow over the pages of a book? This tan apartment with a view of the parking lot didn't feel like a real home.

But more importantly, the first order of business was to get a job. Where to start? Her parents didn't own a computer so she'd have to walk to the nearby library and do a job search there.

"I'm going to the library," she announced to her mother who was smoking a cigarette and scrolling through the list of shows on the television.

Her mother looked up. "Why?"

She scanned the apartment which didn't have any books or magazines. "I'm going to do a job search and check out books."

Sabrina's mother's brows raised.

Was she surprised by the search or the books or both?

"They're hiring at the pet food warehouse." Her mother blew out a smoke ring. "We're leaving so they'll need more help." She flicked an ash onto the scarred table.

Sabrina vaguely remembered them telling her they had jobs there on one of their infrequent visits. She also knew they were leaving soon to return to Detroit to live with Sabrina's grandparents and "help."

Sabrina wasn't sure how helpful they would be. More like they would help themselves to what little her grandparents actually had, including their medications.

They probably planned on living there until they exhausted the grandparents' funds before moving on. In prison, Sabrina had met women with similar motives. They exploited the weak and profited from their misfortune. Her parents were similar. Sabrina had learned about dysfunctional families in counseling, and, no doubt, hers fit the description.

She was happy to leave the smoke-filled apartment and walk to the library, breathing in deeply as she went—enjoying her newfound freedom. She tucked her hands in her pockets and made note of the children riding bikes or throwing a ball. Sabrina remembered doing something similar as a kid, but again, her memories seemed to be filtered through a screen that made them seem like a fantasy...or a dream? Her thoughts had changed three hundred and sixty degrees since the accident and her stay in prison.

At the library, Sabrina applied to the pet food warehouse on-line and was accepted. Her parents had been helpful in that regard. She also selected a couple of books to read while she waited for her job orientation.

When she returned to the apartment, her mother was still sitting on the couch, watching television and her father was scrolling through his phone. They both eyed the books in her arms.

"Since when did you like to read?" Her mother's voice was accusatory like reading was a bad thing.

Shrugging, Sabrina said, "In prison. I read a lot, especially while I was working on my GED and associate's degree."

"You going to stay here when we're gone?" her mother asked, surveying the overflowing ashtray. Her mother struggled off the couch and went into the kitchen.

Sabrina followed her into the tiny kitchen as her mother surveyed the cupboards. Sabrina noted most of the pans were battered, and the dishes were mismatched, chipped, or cracked.

"I guess," Sabrina said, tucking her hands in her back pockets. She had learned in prison to be self-sufficient. "Sure."

"You know..." her father began, "You could go

with us. We'll probably hit the road tomorrow."

"Dad… You know I can't leave."

"Why the hell not?"

She rolled her eyes. "I'm on parole!" *And I have a job now.*

"Oh, yeah." He looked at the ceiling and smacked his palm against his forehead.

Sabrina twisted her fingers together out of restlessness and couldn't wait for her job to start. Being with her parents was depressing. "So, tomorrow?" she asked.

"Maybe tomorrow, maybe not, but soon," her dad said, stroking the stubble on his chin before popping something in his mouth and reaching for another beer.

"You can stay if you want," her mother said again. She shrugged her right shoulder as she talked. "We're current on the rent anyways."

That was a surprise.

Sabrina settled back on the couch and surveyed the sparsely furnished apartment. There was several months of dust on the windowsills and an overflowing ashtray spilled tiny volcanos on the tables. As depressing as this place was, she was free! She could endure almost anything after being locked up.

She spent the night on the lumpy couch that smelled of urine. Disgusting, yes, but she'd smelled urine in prison too.

When her parents left, she reasoned she could clean the place so it smelled better. How long would the manager let her stay? Maybe the halfway house for female ex-prisoners would have openings when she got kicked out?

She loved her parents, but they were on different

paths. She absolutely didn't want to get involved with drugs again. Sabrina decided in prison to make something better for herself. So when they were packed and ready to leave for Detroit, she kissed them goodbye—her father already smelling like a bar and her mother, a stale ashtray. Yes, she loved them, but she didn't like their lifestyle.

"You got this?" Her mother's words were a last-ditch effort at being a responsible parent.

"I learned to take care of myself in prison."

"Call us if you need anything," her mom said.

"Except money," her dad said with a snort. He tossed a key to her. She caught it and stuffed it in her front pocket.

She forced a smile. "Good one, Dad."

She knew she wouldn't call.

Chapter 6

Sabrina waved as her parents shut the door. Letting the smile drop from her face, she thought *Good riddance*! She didn't want to leave Clearwater. First, she hadn't wanted to move here, and now she didn't want to leave.

Go figure.

Plus, she was on parole—she couldn't just up and leave. Of course, she had an ulterior motive—to see Henry and his little girl. The girl must be close to five or six now. Instead of forgetting about them, she felt compelled to wonder and dream about them. Was that normal?

She hadn't felt "normal" since she had awoken from the coma in the hospital. She had all sorts of strange dreams. Not nightmares, but nice dreams, the kind other girls experienced, not her. They had a dream-like quality anyway but seemed almost like memories.

She peeked out the window and saw her parents' battered car chug out of the parking lot spewing black smoke. Would it even make it to Detroit without breaking down?

She shot the deadbolt on the door. She was alone in the apartment at last. She opened the windows to let in some fresh air. She leaned close to the windows breathing deeply, planning what to do next.

Her parents had left the furniture. Sabrina sat on the couch and opened the box her parents had saved for her. On top were some school pictures of Sabrina with an enormous grin missing her two front teeth. Then, some report cards saying she daydreamed and didn't stay on task in class.

Well, she certainly wasn't daydreaming or off-task now. She had her GED certificate and AA degree to prove it.

She shoved the old report cards aside and found a rattle that seemed to have lost its sound. For some reason, her mother thought to save it. And a bib with "Daddy's girl" embroidered on the front. Then, she dug deeper and there was a raggedy baby blanket that was missing part of the bunting at the edge.

At the bottom were too-small jeans and some holey sweatshirts. She'd keep the baby stuff and pictures and toss the rest. On second thought, she'd keep the sweatshirts and use them for apartment cleaning rags.

****

The following day, after eating breakfast, she took her backpack and went to the library. Although she had technically lived here for six years, they were mostly spent behind bars. Clearwater was small, but green signs pointed the way to the center of town and its amenities—library, courthouse, police and public safety department, schools, and the DMV.

Sabrina walked slowly, remembering what she could from before her time in prison, and soon she found herself standing before the Clearwater High School.

She had attended Clearwater, although "attended" might not clearly explain her involvement. She often

31

cut classes and smoked behind the building with Danny.

She vaguely remembered the dark, wild-haired Danny with sunken eyes that seemed flat and lifeless as a lizard. He had visited her in the hospital—slinking in when the guard went to the restroom.

"Don't rat me out!" he had warned, shaking a finger in her direction. "Don't tell them where you got the goods."

She assumed he meant drugs. Already, her mind was drifting away from her old life and the people involved before the accident...

She did remember the guard demanding to know who Danny was when she returned to the room.

"Wrong room." Danny had muttered and backed away, continuing to glare at Sabrina.

Wrong person—wrong room. *Wrong life,* she thought.

****

Now, Sabrina stood before the school and figured Danny was long gone from here. The American flag snapped and waved in the breeze. Sabrina remembered all the details of the building and the surrounding grounds.

Her eyes stopped on the trailer that advertised "Adult Education" and the sign, "Walk-ins Welcome." That building was very familiar, and she felt compelled to take several steps forward. A couple more until she was at the juncture of the driveway—one way led to the main building and the other to the adult education trailer.

Her mind went to the inside of the trailer classroom. Although there wasn't anything spectacular about the inside—the usual plethora of classroom furniture—a flood of memories assailed her. She was so intent on remembering she didn't hear a car approach.

"Can I help you?" a voice called.

The voice startled her, and she turned toward a security guard and his black and white car.

"Uh, no. I used to work here."

He cocked his brow.

When she realized she had misspoken, she flapped her hands by her sides. "I mean, I used to go to school here."

"All visitors must get a pass," he said plainly.

"I'm not staying."

She nodded to him, turned back toward the road, and continued to her original destination—the library.

She passed the playground and park and inhaled green grass smells and a cold, fresh breeze—better than any air freshener. She slowed, passing the play equipment and observing mothers and fathers with their children. The sing-song voices and giggles made her smile.

A man with his back to her looked vaguely familiar. Was that Henry Comstock and his little girl? He turned slightly and she saw his profile. Yes! She was right.

Henry called to a blonde-haired girl. "Maxi! Time to go."

Maxi. Henry's daughter was named Maxi.

Should she make her presence known to them? She thought better of it and stepped back, her body partially hidden by a tree. Sabrina saw Maxi give Henry a hug when she left the jungle gym and bounded over to him—her tiny head thrown back with laughter.

How wonderful it would be to feel the love of a child—Maxi's love in particular.

She longed to hug Maxi and have Maxi wrap her little arms around Sabrina's body. But this puzzled her. She had never cared about little kids before. But Maxi was all she could think about in prison.

Why the attraction?

The love she saw in Maxi's eyes for Henry tugged at her, and she wanted to run toward them and enjoy the embrace—just the three of them.

Chapter 7

Sabrina's parole officer was a woman named Becki—not Becky with a "Y." No, Becki with an "I." Becki was a big, beefy woman with a sleeve of tattoos on her arms and tiny glasses perched on her nose.

"Okay, so, Sabrina." She looked down at the folder on the desk in front of her. "You were paroled two weeks ago. What have you been doing?"

Honestly, did she want to know I cleaned the apartment from top to bottom and threw out all the ashtrays? She answered with "I've been looking for jobs" instead.

"Have you gotten one yet?" Becki asked.

"Yes. I start at the pet food warehouse tomorrow."

"Good." Becki smiled. "Good. That should keep you out of trouble."

Sabrina nodded but remained quiet. She had learned in prison not to run her mouth and to listen.

Becki continued firing questions at her. "Place to live?"

Sabrina shrugged. "I'm at my parents' former apartment for now. They took off for Detroit."

"I see." Becki frowned and picked up a card from her desk. "Here's the number for the halfway house and also to the women's shelter. You can stay there if you need to."

Becki moved her mouth as if considering what to

say next before she continued with the questions. "Are you hanging with your former friends?"

Sabrina shook her head.

What friends?

She hadn't been here long enough to cultivate friends except Danny, and he didn't count as a friend. He sold her drugs and abused her body when she couldn't pay.

"No friends," she mumbled.

"So many people go back to their former way of life, and it's hard to keep a job or obligations."

"Yes, ma'am."

She had only lived in Clearwater three months before the accident changed her life.

Becki tilted her glasses and studied the paperwork on the desk. "You have twenty-five thousand in restitution to pay to the court."

"I know." Her stomach dropped momentarily. That number hung over her head, the dollar amount seemingly endless and unobtainable, but with a job, she reminded herself, it was doable. It might take her two or three years to pay it all, but it was doable.

The "pre-prison" Sabrina hadn't been good with money. As soon as she had some…poof! It was gone. A memory of furtively going through her mother's purse for loose change to buy a hit of meth was all she could remember when it came to money.

No, she hadn't been good at keeping money. She vowed she'd be better this time.

Becki continued. "You'll meet with me on one of your days off and go to a group parolee counseling session at the library."

Becki recited what Sabrina needed to do. "I'll be

checking your work record and also with the court about your restitution. You need to stay clean and take a drug test once a month."

The following day, Sabrina took the bus to the pet food warehouse for paperwork, her schedule, and orientation. While there, she was told where to buy steel-toed boots, some gloves, and an apron before the supervisor explained she would first obtain a packing order, then take the pet food from the conveyor belt and package it in boxes for shipping.

The job required some lifting—fifty pounds—and she'd have Thursdays and Sundays off. That sounded okay to her, and she liked the pay. She'd be able to pay her restitution in about three years and have food to eat and pay rent.

She bought herself a throwaway phone so work could call if they had overtime, as she requested. And she could check in with her parole officer or she could contact her parents, but there wasn't anyone else to call. She would have liked to talk to Henry, but that might be awkward.

On the first day, she trained with a woman named Pat. Pat was a no-nonsense type of woman with short, tightly permed gray hair and a perpetual frown.

"This is what you have to do. Take the bags or cans of food and place them in these boxes"—she pointed to a stack of already-assembled boxes that sat on a conveyor belt—"apply the labels and tape together and then it's ready for shipping. Easy, right?"

Sabrina nodded.

It looked easy, but the conveyor belt kept going, and she ended up having to hurry to grab all the needed packages for a shipment. Kind of like the conveyor belt of life. She snorted—things continued whether you were ready or not.

Sabrina put the dog food into the box, but the treat container continued down the conveyor belt. "I missed the treats!" she grumbled.

"You're fine," Pat said. "If you miss something, it'll come around again."

Sabrina closed her eyes and, in her mind, pictured Henry and Maxi. The thought instantly calmed her and when she opened her eyes, she could cope with the stress. She grabbed the dog treats—they came back around, just like Pat had said—and put them in the box with the food.

Little by little, she learned how to grab all the packages and wrestle them into the box, and her days began to resemble each other.

On Thursdays, she attended a support group for recently released prisoners that, luckily, met at the library basement. The support group was fairly small and run by a man with long white hair—a Charlie Daniels' lookalike named Chuck, who went to prison for embezzlement. *Go figure.*

Everyone in the group seemed to work at the pet food factory. Sabrina recognized several faces. They were one of the few places that employed ex-felons. She wasn't exactly sure why she needed the support group, but it was a condition of parole.

When they finished talking about Al-Anon, family issues, and how hard it was after prison, the session officially ended and allowed Sabrina to go to the main library. She would get a book, spend a couple of hours reading, and then maybe head to the park.

She perused the shelves, looking for the perfect

book, and covertly watched as a woman set up what looked to be story time. The featured books sat on a tripod. Kids' books were colorful, and this one had a cover of unicorns and flowers.

The kids followed a parent helper into the library as Sabrina pulled books from the shelf to read the descriptions on the back.

With one eye on the book and the other on story time, one little girl with blonde hair and blue eyes caught Sabrina's attention. She didn't know what it was about that girl that made her breath stick in her throat, but it did.

The woman began story time with a smile and clap. "I'm Martha. Who are you?" As if the children knew the routine—which they probably did—they called off their names: Suzy, Marie, Kevin, Jacci, Linda, and Maxi. Martha pointed to each child as they said their name. Maxi. The little blonde girl was Maxi—Henry Comstock's daughter.

Sabrina tapped her chin with her forefinger as if doing so would tell her about the girl. Sabrina had seen her at the park with Henry. An invisible bond seemed to stretch between Sabrina and Maxi—a tug so strong it bordered on an obsession.

While in prison, when she had trouble sleeping or was in a stressful situation, she often thought about them—Henry and Maxi. The thought instantly calmed her so she could sleep or handle the situation.

As much as she wanted to sit next to Maxi and put her arm around the girl, Sabrina stayed behind the book stacks. She could see through the volumes and studied Maxi as she listened with her head tipped back, giving the storyteller, Martha, her attention. Sabrina saw Maxi shift and wiggle in her seat. When Martha got to a suspenseful part, Maxi's mouth opened, her eyes wide with concern. But with most kids' books, there was a satisfactory ending, and Maxi clapped along with the others and begged for more.

Maxi—the girl with no mother because of Sabrina. Is that why Sabrina wanted to hug and comfort Maxi the way a mother would? Did Sabrina feel responsible for the little girl? Was that why she couldn't look away and had an indescribable feeling in the pit of her stomach of longing and love and something else she had never experienced before?

When the children left, Martha put the picture book on the table. Sabrina picked up the book and sat in a chair to reread it. Would she ever have a chance to tell Maxi she had read the book about the unicorn who was allergic to the flowers, making her sneeze? She hoped so.

She put the book back on the shelf, checked out her books, and returned to the apartment.

Chapter 8

On Sabrina's days off, when she had no parole requirements, she walked to the in-town park, as it was called. She wasn't sure if it was actually called the in-town park or if it was just something the locals called it, but she hadn't seen a sign indicating another name.

It had all the equipment for a park—swings, slides, a climbing gym that ran the gamut of rings, a climbing wall, a circular slide—and a covered picnic area. When the weather turned warm, she could imagine sitting under the patio cover, reading, and watching the playground activity. It was at this very park that she had learned Maxi's name.

There was trampled snow under the swings and the imprints of tiny boots with zig-zag patterns on the soles. Were those Maxi's footprints? Did Henry and Maxi come here often? It was winter, so maybe not.

As she sat swaying back and forth on the swing in the mostly deserted playground, a gray compact car pulled up, and a man and little girl got out. The girl wore a puffy pink jacket and a hat with sparkly pom-poms. The sequins caught the sunlight and made the hat shine and twinkle. As they came closer, she recognized Henry.

He wore a heavy jacket, but his head was bare, and the light breeze ruffled his hair. He was handsome in an average sort of way—square jaw, direct eyes, and a long nose. He looked like a model for outdoor gear—ruggedly good-looking, but an ordinary-type of guy. She felt a little gasp in the back of her throat.

They stopped when they saw her. She lowered her head to show she was harmless and wouldn't bother them if they didn't want to engage with her.

"Hello," Henry said slowly, cautiously, as he stopped and gave her a peculiar look as if he was trying to put a name to a face.

"Hi."

They looked at each other in silence. Sabrina had so much she wanted to say, yet nothing came out and her mind was an empty vessel.

"Is…is this your little girl?" she asked, breaking the silence. A lame question—asking about the obvious.

He patted the girl's puffy jacket. "Yes, Maxi."

"Daddy! Can I play on the slide?" Maxi looked at her father and glanced briefly at Sabrina, tilting her head slightly.

He nodded as she ran off, and he took the swing next to Sabrina. "I see you got out."

"Yes, a couple of months ago." Sabrina gripped the steel chain holding the swing. "Thank you for what you said at the parole board."

"I did some stupid stuff at seventeen, too." Henry smirked. "You got your GED and associate degree?"

Sabrina nodded. "Again, thank you."

Silence stretched between them. It felt like forever, but it was only a couple of seconds.

Was he getting the restitution payments? "I've been paying the court." She looked at him, but he was looking toward the slide and not her.

"Yes, I got a couple of checks."

"I have a temporary job at the pet food distribution warehouse." She pushed back with her feet and made the swing move.

"How's that?"

She shrugged and continued swinging. "It's a job." But she had already received a weekly award for not missing a day since she began working there.

"True."

"Not my dream job, but that'll never happen."

Only then did he turn to look at her, and she felt her cheeks redden. He didn't need to know.

"And what is that?" he asked, pushing gently on the swing and letting it take him forward and back. Their swings were in sync after a few well-timed pushes.

"A teacher," she said.

"Ah." He seemed to be considering his words. "My wife was a teacher."

Sabrina opened her mouth to speak but they were interrupted by Maxi. Maxi ran up and threw her arms around Henry. With her hat about to fall off, cheeks pink from the cold, she suddenly became shy and whispered loudly, "Daddy! Who's that lady?"

Sabrina wondered what he would tell her. Maxi stood before them and stared at Sabrina in the curious way children sometimes did. Sabrina stopped swinging and smiled at the girl. "I'm Sabrina."

"Oh!" Maxi said.

Another car pulled up behind Henry's, and some kids ran toward the playground, distracting Maxi.

Sabrina then turned to watch Henry, who opened his mouth as if gulping for air before turning to her with a helpless shrug. "Hmm. What do I tell her?" he asked in a low voice.

The truth?

"Is she your friend, Daddy?" Maxi asked, but her eyes followed the other children to the slide.

Sabrina suppressed a giggle, and Henry glared at her—not a mean glare but a look of "don't you laugh at this absurd situation."

"Sorry," Sabrina said and let out her breath. "I don't know what to say either."

Honesty was best, she figured and said, "We don't know each other. I caused the accident your parents were in a few years ago. I wanted to tell him how sorry I was for my actions."

Maxi frowned and said, "It's good to say sorry at school, too." Maxi continued to study Sabrina in a way that made Sabrina want to wipe at her face in case she had dirt on her cheeks or something. "You're pretty."

"Uh, thank you."

Maxi's comment caused her to pause. She hadn't thought about her looks in years. Was she pretty? Her hair was long and unruly at times, and she wore little to no makeup. The next time she was in front of a mirror, she would need to assess her face.

Henry mouthed, "Thanks," as Maxi turned abruptly toward the jungle gym. "Can I go play?"

At least Maxi hadn't questioned her further and seemed to accept the explanation.

"I am sorry," she said quietly. "I wish I could take back my actions." She felt tears well. "I better go." She used the back of her glove to wipe her eyes.

"Will you come again?" he asked. "I like to bring Maxi here so I can have some one-on-one time with

44

her."

"Maybe." Sabrina gave a noncommittal shrug. "My days off are Thursdays and Sundays."

"Okay." Henry nodded. "Maybe we'll see you?" He beckoned Maxi over to the swings.

"I'd like that."

Sabrina waved to Maxi before reluctantly walking away. She didn't want to leave but sensed Henry might want time with Maxi by the way his eyes darted to the slide. She'd go to the library and read for a while, but she'd probably daydream about Henry and Maxi.

****

At the library, Sabrina asked the librarian if they had yearbooks from Clearwater High School.

"A whole section of them," she responded, "going back sixty-two years. I'll show you."

The tall, thin books in various muted colors lined a bottom shelf, so Sabrina sat on the floor and looked through the yearbooks, starting with the last year she had attended.

She flipped to the junior section but didn't see her name, face, or even Danny's. Next, she looked at the pictures of teachers. Most of them were familiar. One in particular was a woman named Marilyn. *We were friends.*

Whoa! That thought seems out-of-character. Friends with a teacher? Hardly.

She continued perusing the pictures until she got to Alison Larkin. She wasn't Alison Comstock yet. Sabrina guessed she had kept her maiden name. The newspaper reported her as Alison Comstock in their write-up of the accident.

Alison was listed as the Adult Education teacher.

Who had Alison been before the accident? She had married Henry, a former student. That was unusual, she thought. What caused a woman...She looked back at the picture of Alison. What caused a woman in her...Sabrina guessed she had to be in her thirties...What caused a woman in her thirties to fall in love with a student in his early twenties?

The situation seemed highly unusual to her. There must be more to their love story, she guessed. Sabrina tapped her chin with her finger. The lack of an answer gnawed at her. Why? Or, more importantly, why did it matter?

She continued to contemplate Alison and Henry's romantic situation until the lights blinked, indicating the library would be closing. Sabrina reluctantly closed the yearbook, put it back, and left without checking out a book—an uncharacteristic gesture.

She walked back to the Heritage Apartments and let herself in and breathed in the pine-scented air—all traces of smoke gone.

Sabrina fixed ramen noodles for dinner and ate a banana. She tapped her fingers on the scarred table and ate slowly while considering her attraction to Henry, Alison, and Maxi. Was it normal? Perhaps she'd ask others at the support group if they obsessed over their victims. Somehow though, Sabrina thought her situation was unusual. She didn't know why she thought that, but she did.

Chapter 9

At group, Sabrina surprised herself by raising her hand.

"Sabrina?" Chuck asked. "Do you have a question?"

"Yes." Her voice faltered, and her words seemed stuck in her throat. She cleared it and swallowed. "Does everyone feel remorse about their victims?"

Several people nodded, but several studied their feet as if embarrassed.

Chuck looked around the circle. "Anyone want to answer Sabrina?"

A woman raised her hand. "I've regretted what I did and still do."

"Does anyone think about them weekly?" Sabrina asked.

The same woman nodded.

"I was seventeen," Sabrina swallowed, "when I caused the accident that killed Alison Comstock."

Chuck's head swiveled as he looked at the group.

A man raised his hand as if to ask permission and said, "You were young."

"I took drugs," Sabrina said.

Nobody spoke. Several others nodded.

So, were they saying because of her age, it was okay to take drugs and drive?

"I think about the man and his daughter all the

time!" Sabrina blurted out.

A couple of people frowned.

"Is that normal?"

The woman who confirmed her regret said, "I don't think of them all the time. From time to time or something will trigger those memories." She turned to Sabrina. "You should see someone about that."

Chuck raised his brows. "I would have to agree."

Who was she to see about her obsession with Henry and Maxi? She guessed deep down in her heart she knew there was something different about her situation. She thought she loved them, even though she didn't know them. Was that normal?

"Ok," she squeaked, "thanks."

Chuck took a card from his pocket and wrote something down before handing it to her. "Here's the number of a counselor who can help you sort out your feelings about your victims."

Sabrina took the card, her face pink with embarrassment, and shoved it in her pack.

Chuck began their session, and everyone turned their attention to other concerns the parolees had.

Chapter 10

After work on Monday, Sabrina took the bus back to the library and met with the teacher and a group of women working on their GEDs. Several attendees were doing so because of court orders and part of their parole—they needed to finish their education. Some were enthusiastic, and others went through the motions.

But as her grandfather used to say, "You can lead a horse to water, but you can't make him drink." No matter, helping made Sabrina feel better about herself and pushed her obsession with Henry and Maxi aside.

The GED program didn't have a wide range of books like the prison, but the women could check books out from the library if they wished. Each woman practiced reading and answering questions about the text from dog-eared workbooks.

The woman she was working with today was named Natalie, and her wispy red hair danced around her head as if she had static electricity on her scalp. Sabrina smiled at Natalie to begin, and Natalie began to read haltingly from the passages in the workbook.

Little by little, Natalie's reading improved, and she could retain what she read and answer all the questions about the passages.

Sabrina could understand why some women couldn't remember what they had read. The paragraphs were bland and dry. Who cared what was on sale at the fictional grocery store? Couldn't someone write passages that were interesting to read? Maybe she could do that someday…

When Sabrina finished tutoring, she wanted to breathe fresh air and walk to the park. But it was late March in Michigan and late March could mean storm-warning gray, overcast days or marginal sunshine, rain, snow, sleet, or hail. Michigan could get it all in a span of a few days.

The shade of night was falling, and the lights over the park were lit with an unnatural yellow glow. The park was mostly empty except for a few dark outlines standing under the picnic awning where a child skipped rope and the adults were smoking or talking. Sabrina rubbed her arms, did a cursory search for Maxi and Henry, and was about to turn away when a familiar gray car pulled up. Henry Comstock. A little chill ran up her arms.

She watched Maxi bound from the car with Henry close behind, running to catch up. Would it feel weird if she followed them? She took in a gulp of chilled air and followed Henry to the swing set. Maxi was already at the slide by the climbing wall. Since Sabrina had technically been at the park first, maybe it wasn't so odd she was here again when they were.

"Hello," she said, and Henry jerked his head up and peered at her in the deepening gloom. "I hope I'm not disturbing you. I was taking a walk."

Henry sat on one of the swings. "You're not disturbing us."

"I know your time must be precious with her."

Henry looked up and blinked—a puzzled look creased his brow.

"You know, being a busy doctor and all."

"Yes."

Henry seemed to be studying his feet, and Sabrina wondered if he had a lot on his mind. Did she know what kind of doctor he was? E.R. she guessed. Serving in the E.R. would be stressful with car accidents, shootings, and drug overdose victims, etc.

She sat on the swing next to him, gently moving back and forth, and periodically watching Maxi climb up and down the equipment. Maxi waved to her and Sabrina felt her heart swell at the girl's attention.

Henry's voice startled her momentarily.

"The park helps Maxi calm down so when we get home she can do her homework." He kicked off the ground slightly and the swing swayed back and forth. "She's cooped up most of the day at school, so this is good for her. We only stay fifteen or twenty minutes but it helps her run off some energy."

The fresh air was good for Sabrina, too, after working in the warehouse. "I understand."

When Maxi finished, she ran over to them. "Hi!"

"Hi, yourself!" Sabrina said, giving Maxi a big smile. "How are you?"

Maxi moved a foot back and forth in the wood chips that lined the playground equipment.

"Pretty good." Maxi moved closer to the swings.

"You're getting so big." Sabrina had only seen Maxi a dozen or so times, first at her trial when she was a baby wrapped in a pink blanket.

"I'm in first grade." Maxi straightened her back.

"Really? Are you reading?"

Maxi nodded her head. "I love to read!"

Henry nodded too, like any proud parent would,

and said, "She's actually reading at a third-grade level."

"That's wonderful," Sabrina said. "I love to read too." Should she share that she saw Maxi during story time at the library? She didn't want to be a stalker or anything, but it was a small town with only so many places to go. They were bound to run into each other now and then.

"We should probably go," Henry said, looking at his watch.

"No!" Maxi said, "I want to go on the slides again!"

"Okay, but only five more minutes."

He continued to swing and so did she. Sabrina wasn't sure what to say to him. Should she ask about work?

"How was work today?"

He paused, but didn't seem surprised by her question. "The usual." He shrugged. "Stitched up people who were hurt."

Stitching up people was usual?

His voice was mellow and deep and Sabrina could imagine patients felt comforted by his voice alone. She knew she was and she wasn't a patient.

Suddenly, Henry stood, stretched his back, and looked around. "Did you drive?"

"No, I don't have a car. I walked here."

He turned to Sabrina. "Would you like a ride home? It's getting dark." He called out to Maxi, "Time to go!"

And it was. The people under the awning had left and it was only the three of them. The sounds of cars quieted, and there were no screeching tires or horns. Most people were already home from work and eating dinner.

Usually, the dark didn't bother her—she could be anonymous and blend in with the night but Henry's gesture was touching. It was so like him.

That thought caused her to stop and consider her words. How did she know that about him? Was it the way he had defended her at her parole hearing?

She grabbed her pack and followed Maxi and Henry to the car. "I'm not far. Just the Heritage Apartments," she said.

"Oh." Henry ran his hand through his hair. "We don't mind, do we?" he asked Maxi, but Maxi was already opening the car door and getting into her booster seat. Henry opened the passenger door and inclined his head.

Impulsively, when he stopped at the apartments she said, "If you need a babysitter for Maxi, let me know."

His brows knitted as he squinted at her in the small light above the console. "You want to babysit Maxi?"

"Yes, Daddy!" Maxi squealed from the backseat. "I want Sabrina to babysit! We can go to the park!" Maxi clapped her hands together. "Grandma doesn't like to go to the park!"

Sabrina was surprised by Maxi's enthusiasm. It was almost as if they had a kind of connection.

He dipped his chin. "How do I reach you?"

Besides the park?

He handed her a slip of paper and a pencil where she wrote her phone number. "That's a seven, not four." Her handwriting was messy.

He fished in his pocket, pulled out his wallet, and handed her a business card.

"Thanks for the ride." She left the car, but Henry

didn't immediately drive off. He sat frozen, staring at her telephone number. Was he having second thoughts? She hoped not, tucking his card away in the pocket of her pack for safekeeping.

At the doorway, she turned. He was still there, but she wasn't looking at him—she noticed his license plate, 4EAEA. She knew it must have some meaning. She had seen it before. Sabrina chewed absently on her lip and tried to decipher the letters. 4E could mean 4 ever, but she wasn't sure of the rest. She'd have to remember to ask him what his license meant next time they were at the park.

Somehow, she felt their lives were entangled, not just because of the accident—something else she hadn't yet fathomed. The answers seemed to be nibbling around the edges of her subconscious like curious fish. What was she supposed to know about Henry? And what was the significance of 4EAEA?

Chapter 11

After the counseling session on Thursday, Sabrina went into the main library. One of the other parolees followed her—a man named Billy. She hoped he wasn't going to bother her and deliberately turned into the chick lit section to see if he would. She studied the titles and took three to check out. She saw him hesitate from the corner of her eye before coming toward her.

"Are ·you following me?" she asked, holding the books to her chest like a shield.

"I just wanted to talk with you," Billy said.

He came closer. He had short light-brown hair and an ordinary face. He was skinny, too—hardly threatening, and she felt the tension leave her body.

"I went to prison for breaking and entering," he said. "I was on drugs, but I'm clean now." He held up his hands as if showing her he had surrendered.

She thought she remembered that from the counseling session when they introduced themselves to the other members.

"Why do you tell me that?" she asked. It was an unusual pick-up line.

He shrugged. "You looked afraid of me."

"Hmmm." Maybe she was a little.

"I won't hurt you. I just want to talk to you and tell you some things."

She tilted her head to one side and studied him.

"What things?"

"She was my second cousin."

It took several beats for her to respond. "She?" Sabrina frowned at him until she realized he was talking about Alison. "Alison?"

He nodded.

"I'm sorry." Here was another person impacted by her actions. Billy lost a cousin, albeit a distant one, but still… Did he want to yell at her? Beat her up? "I said I'm sorry."

"I didn't know her. I lived in Wisconsin most of my life. I only returned to Michigan a few years ago."

When he didn't make a threatening move toward her, she relaxed a bit and realized he just wanted to talk, not fight.

"What was she like?" Sabrina asked.

He suddenly seemed interested in the floor and his sneakers. "I didn't know Alison. Heard some stories about her from my mother who was in contact with her mother."

"What sort of stories?" Sabrina leaned back against a shelf.

He paused and narrowed his eyes as if thinking. "I remember my mom telling me Rob kept tasting the Thanksgiving gravy and adding salt until my aunt smacked him with a wooden spoon. I think she had to make a new batch."

Sabrina frowned at him but nodded once.

"I guess you'd have to have been there." Billy waved his hands as if to erase what he just said. "Oh! I've got another story. Alison and her boyfriend—who eventually became her husband—rescued a little girl on the Ferris wheel at Cedar Springs."

An image of a little girl wearing pink shorts skittered across her mind.

He continued, "It made the national news. I remember watching it with my mother and her calling all her friends about her hero cousin."

Sabrina was pulled between listening to Billy and looking for Maxi. Her curiosity got the better of her, and she wanted to know more about Alison.

"Would you like to sit down?" he asked.

She nodded and followed Billy to a table. She could check out books later and waited for him to share more. "Anything else?"

"It's kind of sad, but her husband was killed in a car accident, too. On a foggy night."

Sabrina's mind whirled. Alison had been married before Henry. Did Henry know? She assumed so.

Billy sat staring at her with a quizzical look—narrowed eyes, head tilted to the side—as if she should say something now.

"Er, why are you...you in Clearwater?" she stuttered.

"Long story," he said with a sigh and didn't elaborate further.

Sabrina moved her shoulders around and fingered the books she wanted to check out.

"Do you work at the pet food warehouse, too?"

He chuckled. "Seems like everyone works there. I'm in receiving."

A completely different warehouse, Sabrina knew.

"Packaging and shipping," she replied.

The children filed out after story time. Sabrina missed the opportunity to talk to Maxi. Sabrina let out a sigh. Maxi's head bobbed by and she was whispering to another girl. There was always next week.

Billy must have noticed Sabrina looking at the kids. "Do you know any of them?"

Should she tell him one was Alison's? After all, they were distantly related.

"Not really." Sabrina shrugged. "One of those little girls is Alison and Henry's child, though." She pointed out Maxi.

"Henry? I thought her husband was Rob and that she had a miscarriage?" Billy said, his brows scrunched together.

Now it was Sabrina's turn to be confused. "Who's Rob?"

"Alison's husband. They were high school sweethearts, I think. She was pregnant when he was killed in an auto accident."

Alison was married twice to Rob and Henry.

"But you say she was married to someone named Henry and that's their little girl?"

Billy swiveled in his seat and looked at the children exiting the library, some with parents and others with the storyteller.

"The one with the pink barrettes is Maxi." Sabrina pointed the girl out again.

"Ahhh."

They sat, not talking, until Billy looked at the clock. He left. After Billy's departure, Sabrina checked out a computer to research the Ferris wheel rescue. It sounded intriguing.

When she searched for Cedar Springs, Ferris Wheel, and Rescue, she found the following from the *Clearwater News*:

Local Kids Are Heroes

Two local teens skipping school saved a little girl on the Ferris wheel at Cedar Springs Amusement Park in Sandusky, OH. The park is a favorite for many. Two Clearwater teens were stranded when the Ferris wheel suffered mechanical difficulties and stopped midway through the ride. An unaccompanied girl was frightened and tried to get out of her seat when Robert L, climbed to her side and comforted her until they were rescued by the fire department.

The article was dated twenty years ago. Sabrina sat back as her mind began remembering, almost like an old-time movie—reels of black and white grainy pictures. Had she remembered it from news reports when she was a small child?

She recalled the smells and sounds. Usually, her dreams didn't include popcorn or hot dog smells, or the sounds the rides made when they began or finished. No, these were memories. Memories that weren't hers but were in her head.

When she finished reading all the articles about the rescue, she returned to the shelf of yearbooks and eased herself down to the floor before pulling out some older books, guessing when Alison had been a student. Sabrina ran her fingers down the list of students and their faces, looking for Alison and someone named Robert L.

Robert Larkin.

Her finger stayed pressed to his picture and name. An image of brown, compassionate eyes came to Sabrina—eyes that unlocked her innermost secrets and touched her heart and soul. An overwhelming blanket of sadness settled over her when she remembered those eyes. Why? Henry Comstock's eyes. And she blushed.

"Ooh, girl," she told herself, "methinks you have a little crush!...Shuddup!" she said to herself. "I do not."

She then turned to the sports and clubs section, and there he was again. Turned out, Robert Larkin was a baseball star. Sabrina studied the full-length picture of him in his baseball uniform, holding a bat across his shoulders, looking confident and sure.

She knew he was the boy who rescued the little girl on the Ferris wheel. He looked like the helpful sort of person when he told the girl in the pink shorts, "Sit down. I'm coming for you!"

His stance was confident, but he didn't have a shit-eating grin like some guys she knew. She was sure he was Alison's first husband.

Did she want to look up Alison, too? She wasn't sure she wanted to see Alison in high school—a woman whose potential was cut short by Sabrina's recklessness. No, she wasn't ready to face Alison.

She felt tears dribbling down her cheeks. She cried for Alison and herself. Knowing what she had done was worse than any prison sentence, and she swiped away the tears with the back of her hand. She would never get out on parole. Her remorse would forever be with her, and she would be imprisoned with regrets forever and ever, always.

Chapter 12

The parolee support group was held in the library basement this week because the main floors were closed for carpet cleaning. After their heart-to-heart, Billy began sitting by her.

The counselor asked, "Does anyone have anything they'd like to share?"

One woman raised her hand and screwed her mouth into a sneer. "Yes! I've been let go at the warehouse!"

A ripple went around the circle, and several people shuffled their feet.

"How am I supposed to live if I don't have that job?"

A man raised his hand. "I've heard they're laying off for their slow season but will rehire in the fall."

"That may be," the woman said. "But I've got five months to go and restitution to pay!"

The counselor, Charles asked, "Does anyone know of any jobs in the area?"

Sabrina looked around the circle of people—most were shaking their heads. She had only heard of the warehouse hiring parolees—no other business was so inclined. If that woman lost her job, could the same thing happen to Sabrina? Would she have to leave Clearwater and move to Detroit with her parents? She stifled a shudder at that thought.

"I heard they're hiring truck drivers," a different man said.

The woman who had lost her job scoffed, "How will that help me? I've got kids!"

No one had an answer for her.

Truck driving wouldn't be an option for Sabrina, either. She couldn't get her license for another year.

When the session finished, Sabrina walked up the steps and sighed deeply—so many problems for parolees. She wasn't sure what to do this afternoon. She usually went into the library, returned her books from the previous week, and checked out more, but the library was closed. Should she go back to the apartment and reread one of her books? That thought was depressing.

Most of the parolees left; only Billy remained. "Would you like to get coffee or something?" Billy asked.

"No, it's too late for coffee, I think. Sorry. I'm going to go for a walk."

"Can I walk with you?"

"If you want." Sabrina shrugged. She didn't mind his company—Billy was friendly enough, but she didn't feel anything for him.

They turned left from the library and right into the residential neighborhood that ringed the center of Clearwater. The houses began to get smaller the farther they walked.

Billy stopped at the street signs. "I think Alison's family lived around here someplace. My mom has an envelope with their return address on it."

"Oh?" That didn't really tell Sabrina anything about Alison.

"Anything else?"

"She was a teacher at Clearwater High School."

"Hmm."

How was that information useful as she reconciled her part in the accident? They walked quietly.

"So…" Billy began. "Tell me about yourself?"

Did she want to tell Billy about herself? There wasn't much to tell. Her life appeared dull and bland, like tapioca pudding. Did she have something interesting hiding behind her façade?

"What do you want to know?"

"How'd you end up here?"

She looked around. Maple and Beech Streets. She recognized the neighborhood. "We walked," she said, trying to keep a straight face.

Billy paused before chuckling. "I guess I didn't phrase that right. How did you end up in Clearwater and prison?"

"It's a long story—I don't feel like talking about my past life right now." She tucked her hands into her pockets as they continued along the residential street.

"Of course. I'm sorry for asking."

She had already told her story and didn't want to keep rehashing the past. Besides, everyone had a similar sob story—drugs made them crazy, they made bad choices, everyone came from unstable homes, some had parents who didn't care. Her life story checked all these boxes.

They continued walking until they came to a house with a wide front porch. Sabrina knew the house—blue siding with white columns and lace curtains bordering the windows. She remembered sitting on the porch swing. But how could that be?

Sabrina paused and turned to face it. Her breath wedged painfully in her throat. She swallowed, but still the gagging feeling remained. What was it about this house that made her stop? It was a craftsman style, and they had passed many more like this in different colors—tan, white, brown, grays, and blues. What made this one unusual? It wasn't the outer façade, she reasoned, but the memories contained within...

"Do you know who lives here?" Billy asked, shifting feet as she continued to study the front porch.

She wanted to wave her hands and tell him to "ssh" as she continued studying the house. And as though she had x-ray vision, she could see the blue couch and the chair by the window. She wanted to walk up those steps, let herself in, or at least look through the windows.

"No," she answered. "I don't know who lives here." Currently, she added silently.

Had she once lived here? Her parents hopscotched around from one place to another, outrunning the late rent or threats to turn off the electricity. They usually rented apartments in sketchy parts of town, not residential areas. And certainly not cute, cozy homes like this one.

But she did know this house. She remembered sitting on the couch, the curtains drawn tight, waiting and hearing the faint rustle of bushes. Someone was outside, watching her. A tingle of electricity leapt up her spine, and she shook it off. It was as if she was viewing the scene through the haze of cobwebs—indistinct shapes and movement.

"We better go," she said. "It's cold."

"Are you sure you don't want coffee or hot

chocolate or something?"

"I'm sure." The cold she felt was something her grandmother once said: "A ghost walked over my grave." It was the feeling of knowing something she shouldn't, but she did—a sense of pending doom.

She sincerely hoped Billy wasn't interested in her and was just being nice. He wasn't the guy she wanted to see right now.

She turned away from the house, feeling as if she could cry. Had it been the talk of the warehouse layoffs? Or something else?

****

"Are you okay?" Billy asked.

"Yes, just…just…remembering. Let's go." She turned away, hurrying so she wouldn't have to talk to Billy. When they returned to the library, her breath came in gasps. She had to get away by herself and think. Her first thought was the park.

"Please, Billy, I want to be alone." She hugged herself. She secretly hoped she ran into Henry and Maxi at the park. Seeing Maxi always made her feel better.

He held his arms wide. "Sure. Sorry, you're upset."

"It's not your problem."

It was her problem to solve, but somehow, she was missing some chapters and couldn't jump to the book ending to see how it turned out. She hadn't figured out the riddle of her life's mystery.

Chapter 13

After leaving Billy, she hurried toward the park, hoping to see Henry and Maxi. It was almost five. Would they be there?

What luck. Sabrina saw the silver-gray Toyota with the 4EAEA plates parked by the curb and spotted Henry sitting on the swings, talking to a woman Sabrina didn't recognize. She stopped and analyzed the scene before her when the woman reached out and hugged Maxi and another little girl.

She hadn't even considered Henry might have a girlfriend. Of course he would. Henry was a handsome man—and a doctor. She was sure he could have his pick of any woman he wanted. Her stomach dropped. How could she have been so dumb?

With tears in her eyes, she started to turn away when Maxi looked up and waved. "Sabrina!"

She gave Maxi a smile and wiped her eyes before walking toward the foursome. "Hi." She gave a little wave.

The woman with Henry narrowed her eyes. Sabrina kept the smile plastered on her face as she took in the woman's features—long blonde, bordering on white hair, calculating blue eyes, and a simpering smile.

She wore a pencil skirt and heels to the park. To the park! Sabrina stifled a laugh as she started to walk over.

Henry said, "Olivia, this is Sabrina, Sabrina, Olivia." He struggled out of his swing and moved his hand, indicating that Sabrina should sit.

"His girlfriend," Olivia said and held out her hand as if she wanted Sabrina to kiss it.

"Nice to meet you." Sabrina took Olivia's limp fingers in hers for a lackluster shake.

"And this is Brooklyn," Maxi said, introducing the little girl to her.

Sabrina smiled at the way Maxi said Brooklyn's name. It was obvious by Maxi's downturned lips she didn't like Brooklyn.

"My daughter," Olivia explained.

The resemblance was striking. Brooklyn was her mother's mini-me—corn-silk hair and lashes surrounding cold, glacier-blue eyes, and a pouting mouth.

"I was just passing by and won't stay," Sabrina said, giving the swing a little push.

"That's too bad," Olivia said.

Hmm.

"No!" Maxi said. "Can you push me on the swings?"

"I can do that," Olivia offered.

"I want Sabrina!" Maxi said with a frown. "I thought you were going to babysit me!"

Maxi tugged on Sabrina's arm. "Come on!"

Well...to spite Olivia, Sabrina decided she might stay. But she didn't want to upset Henry, who looked confused by the situation—a crease lined his forehead.

"Soon," Henry said, looking first at Olivia and then at Maxi and shifted feet.

"Maybe I can babysit while your dad and Olivia go

to dinner or something." Sabrina suggested.

Olivia's gaze bore into Sabrina's. Was she upset Sabrina had suggested babysitting? Or the dinner part?

Maxi climbed into the swing, and Sabrina began to push her. Her mind swirled with her stupidity of thinking Henry was hers. He wasn't hers. He was never hers. He would never be hers! *You killed his wife, remember?* she goaded herself. And now he was Olivia's boyfriend!

He couldn't know the way she felt. She didn't know how she felt until now.

There was something she had wanted to talk to Henry about before she got to the park. She chewed on her bottom lip. Her mind was blank as she concentrated on Maxi's back and pushing her.

"Higher!" Maxi giggled.

Sabrina gave it her best push, and Maxi soared higher with a laugh. All the lifting at the warehouse gave her extra strength in her arms.

Even with her voice on low, Sabrina heard Olivia's conversation with Henry. "I thought your mother babysat for her?"

"She's back to work now."

"Can't you find someone else?" Olivia's voice was like an old-time radiator hiss or an angry cat.

Sabrina couldn't hear Henry's reply, his words muffled.

"We'll talk about this later," Olivia huffed.

And by the look on Olivia's face, Sabrina was sure she'd veto the babysitting. A woman recognized another woman's jealousy and possessiveness—a sort of second sense. Sabrina saw that in Olivia. But Sabrina hadn't survived prison by not being assertive. She was drawn to Henry and wasn't going to let Olivia derail her relationship with Maxi. Game on!

"Maybe," Henry said, straightening up and moving his head around.

Sabrina peeked at him from behind her lashes. His tightened mouth told Sabrina something else. He could be assertive too!

Soon Olivia clapped, "Time to go, girls!"

Sabrina stopped pushing Maxi and waited for the swing to slow.

"I want to stay!" Maxi said.

Olivia said, "If we're going to the movies, we need to go now." Her mouth pursed in a tiny smile at Maxi's request.

Strangely, Henry was quiet, his arms folded.

Ah, Sabrina concluded by their body language, not everything was right in paradise.

"Come on, Maxi." Henry sighed. "We gotta go," he told Sabrina and mouthed "Sorry" as he turned to follow Olivia.

Maxi hopped off her swing to grab her dad's hand. She turned back to look at Sabrina and asked, "See you soon?"

"I hope so," Sabrina said as she watched them leave the playground and get into Henry's car. Her emotions were hard to describe—fear and desire, rolled into a tight knot in her stomach.

Fear licked like a flame at her knowing she might lose Maxi. Puzzled that her desire for Henry was growing, and that she needed them both in her life somehow.

Chapter 14

Sabrina worked on Friday, and that morning, the personnel department began calling in workers individually. Sabrina watched with growing dread as her co-workers left and came back—their faces stony and grim. Again, she felt the tell-tale shiver down her spine. A ghost walked over her grave again—the dreaded layoffs had begun in her department.

"What's going on?" she asked, even though she had heard about the staff reduction.

"Layoffs," the nearest worker said.

"All of us?" Sabrina asked.

"Temporary staff first," she said adjusting the bandana around her head.

Sabrina felt her insides turn to slush. She was a temporary worker. Would she be next? Truck driving? Was that her only option? She didn't even have a license! And the thought of getting behind the wheel again...Well, it scared her shitless.

If she was laid off, then what? How would she pay Henry? Or keep the apartment? How would she eat?

"When?" Sabrina asked.

"They're staggering it," the woman confirmed.

Sabrina hadn't gotten to know her co-workers well.

It had been a temporary job when she signed on, but after five months, it felt permanent, and she was paying off what she owed Henry.

"Sabrina Timmons."

Sabrina gulped, removed her work gloves, shoved them in her pockets, and walked toward the management offices.

The woman behind the desk had her computer on and was scrolling through names and faces.

She stopped by the desk, cleared her throat, and said, "I'm Sabrina Timmons."

The woman wore tiny reading glasses and moved her head up and down as she studied the computer and the papers on the desk.

"I hate to lay you off with your perfect attendance record," she said.

"But?" Sabrina chewed at a piece of chapped skin on her lips.

The woman rubbed the bridge of her nose. "But I can't help it; business slows down at this time of the year. Can we call you to work during vacation season when many workers are gone?"

"Yes, I need this job." Sabrina gulped. "I need to pay my restitution to the court."

"Okay," the woman said. "I'll put you down as available for work as a substitute. I'm sorry I don't have better news. You'll work the next two weeks, but we'll pay you for three. Maybe you can get unemployment."

"Do...do you know of other places hiring?"

The woman shook her head and pressed a button on the computer. "I'm sorry, I don't. You can search online."

"Thanks." Sabrina nodded before turning to leave. She'd be out of a job in two weeks. She had a thousand dollars saved. Would she have to send it to the court instead of paying for the apartment? Would she end up in the halfway house or the women's shelter? Neither option sounded optimal.

She returned to her station, nodded grimly to the woman with the bandana, and began grabbing cans and bags of pet food off the conveyor belt and placing them in boxes for shipping. She felt her lips quiver several times, but she didn't want to cry. Not here. *Later*, she promised herself, later, she could cry into her pillow at the unfairness of it all.

****

That evening after work, she went to the library to check out a computer and study the job postings: pet sitting, childcare, part-time janitorial, and bus driving—nothing that paid like the warehouse though. And would she be able to pass the background check for childcare? Her options were limited.

She turned off the computer and took one of the books she had selected for check out and sat in one of the chairs by the windows. She'd lose herself in the latest paranormal romance about a reincarnated couple whose love story spanned hundreds of years. The book was interesting, and she liked learning about their past lives during WWII and the Civil War.

She began reading until she felt a jolt and jerked upright. The lights were flickering signaling the library was closing. "Uh!" She must have fallen asleep.

Lately, she hadn't been sleeping well. Not with the layoffs hanging over everything. *Well*, she thought with a frown, *that's not hanging there anymore; it's a sure thing*.

The next night after work she repeated the routine. She went to the library to do another job search. Several new jobs were listed.

Clearwater Elementary School needed a special education aide. That would have been a perfect job for her, but it required fingerprints, a background check, and clean driving record. Maybe they would overlook her prison record?

She continued scrolling down the list since she didn't have a clean driving record or a clean background. A warehouse in Muskegon was hiring, but it would require an almost hour ride on the bus. It might work if that was the only thing she could find.

The job search was depressing: flower arranging for half what she was making at the warehouse, a food truck worker, a postal worker...Nope. She continued looking at the list. Nope. Nope. Nope.

Sabrina got up from the computer, stretched, and hesitated before looking at the yearbook section again. Sighing, she retrieved the yearbook with the pictures of Robert Larkin, Alison's boyfriend and eventual husband.

There were many pictures of Robert "Rob" Larkin in the book. He was the baseball star and seemed to be friends with everyone. Most of the images of him were with Alison. Rob and Alison at the Christmas Dance. Rob and Alison during Homecoming. Rob and Alison donating blood for the Honor Society.

Sabrina sat with her back against the wall and kept the yearbook open on her lap. She couldn't figure out the age difference between Alison and Henry. Sabrina did a rough calculation. They had to be about twelve years apart—but who was she to judge?

Alison was a beautiful woman in her thirties and looked just as youthful as she did in her teens. Why was it okay for older men to be with much younger women? Alison loved Henry, or so she figured, and Sabrina wanted the same thing for herself—a man to love her.

She looked back at the yearbook picture of Rob and Alison at the Christmas dance—their arms around each other, heads touching as if whispering secrets. *Rob was whispering he loved Alison.*

She couldn't be sure, only a knowing that belied reason. Maybe he was saying something else?

She grimaced and wished she wasn't obsessed with Alison. Why? Was it just her remorse at causing Alison's untimely death or something else? She couldn't put her finger on it.

Chapter 15

The parole support group was abuzz with the warehouse layoffs this afternoon.

Billy sat near her again. Sabrina leaned over. "Did you get laid off?" she asked.

"Not yet," he said, "but I expect it. I might have to drive a truck for a while."

That option was out for her, and she quirked a brow at him.

The leader kept raising his hand for quiet. "Please, let's not talk over each other."

"What are we going to do?" one woman whined.

Sabrina surprised herself by saying, "A warehouse in Muskegon is hiring."

A chorus of "what's it called?" and "hiring what?" and "full time?" rang out.

Sabrina wrinkled her nose and thought back to her job search. "Pitneys, I believe. It looked like a good job. I don't know if it's full time, but I think so…"

"Did you apply?" the whiny woman asked.

"I don't have a car"—Sabrina shrugged—"and would have to take the bus there. I don't even know if there's a bus between Clearwater and Muskegon."

"There is, but it will take you almost two hours to get there," someone from the back piped up.

Sabrina watched several people write that information down.

"What are you going to do?" Billy whispered as Chuck hushed everyone.

"I don't know." She pushed back the rising panic and pictured Maxi's sweet face.

Their leader, Chuck, kept raising his hand for quiet, but there was no quieting the group today. Sabrina looked at his frowning, resigned face and let everyone discuss the layoffs.

****

After the session ended early, Sabrina trudged up the steps to the main library. Thankfully, Billy didn't follow her. She didn't want to think about Alison today. All she wanted was to be alone and consider her options—which were severely limited.

So far, all she had was to stay in Clearwater near her parole officer, Becki, and possibly ride a bus four hours daily for another warehouse job. Or get permission to move to Detroit, live with her parents, and find a job there. Neither option appealed to her. Except she knew she had to stay in Clearwater and continue to run into Maxi and Henry at the park.

Sure, she could get unemployment benefits, but it was only half what she was making currently. The situation seemed hopeless.

She did notice there were several nanny positions, but who would hire an ex-felon to care for their kids? She stopped searching to throw her head back. *I would have been so good at taking care of kids!*

She needed something because she was running out of time. She only had a couple of days left to work, and then she was done. What to do? Tell the court she didn't have a job and couldn't make her payments. Did they even care?

Since she couldn't answer her dilemma, she wandered the stacks looking for books to read. She checked out three and sat at one of the tables near the door to get lost in a book, read about other people's problems, and not think about her own.

A gaggle of voices surged toward the door, and Sabrina put down her book and looked toward the children—the story time crowd. When Maxi saw Sabrina sitting there she squealed, making a beeline toward her.

"Sabrina! What are you doing here?" Maxi asked, giving her a shy smile, revealing a missing tooth.

"I have a meeting at the library on Thursdays."

"Oh!" Maxi wrinkled her nose. "Me too."

The rest of the children surged out the door or waited for their parents to pick them up. Who was coming for Maxi?

"Do you have a ride?" Sabrina asked.

"Daddy's supposed to pick me up. But sometimes he's late because of his job. Sometimes Grandma comes." She grimaced and rolled her eyes. "Or Olivia."

Olivia, Henry's girlfriend. The woman at the park who had looked at Sabrina with predatory eyes.

Sabrina pushed her books aside and patted the chair next to her. "You can wait with me."

"I have homework," Maxi said. "But I'm hungry. I wish he'd hurry."

"Should we get something from the vending machine?" Sabrina asked. She knew four machines near the restrooms dispensed chips, granola bars, candy, juice, water, and pop.

Maxi pouted. "I don't have any money."

Sabrina reached into the side pocket of her pack

and pulled out some crumpled bills and a handful of coins. "Do you think we can get something with this?" The money was for the bus, but Maxi came first.

Maxi nodded vigorously. "Yes!"

Hand in hand, they went to the machines and selected what Maxi wanted: tiny powdered donuts, gummy fruit snacks, and apple juice. Sabrina bought herself a granola bar so that Maxi wouldn't eat alone.

"Shall we work on your homework?"

Satisfied with her snack and powdered sugar smudging her mouth, Maxi pulled out a dog-eared math workbook.

Maxi reached up and touched Sabrina's cheek, startling her. "What's that on your cheek, Sabrina?"

Instinctively her hand reached up. "It's a scar from my auto accident."

"Daddy has one too. I have one on my knee where I fell off my bike."

"I guess everyone has them," Sabrina said.

Maxi seemed satisfied by the answer, and they worked through the math problems. Sabrina couldn't believe elementary students were doing algebra equations. They were working head to head and whispering when Henry arrived.

"Hello!"

Sabrina jumped and gasped. "Sorry." She placed a hand on her chest. "You startled me."

"Daddy!"

"I didn't mean to. Sorry, I'm late, Maxi."

Maxi shrugged. "That's okay. Sabrina bought me snacks and is helping me with math."

Sabrina snorted. "I can't believe how hard elementary math is."

Henry sagged into a chair opposite them. "I know," he said with a smile. "I feel the same way sometimes."

"I wish Sabrina could help me after school all the time!" Maxi declared.

"I think we could do that on her days off if she wants to," he said, giving her a raised brow look—an unspoken question.

"I'm going to be laid off in two days." She turned slightly and waved her arm over a bank of computers. "I'll have plenty of time if I can't find another job."

Henry tilted his head back as if he was thinking. "Hiring you to tutor Maxi after school might help me and you." He ruffled Maxi's hair. "It's a win-win."

Was he suggesting she work daily with Maxi? She could hardly believe it.

"Well…" he said slowly, "I think I can employ you—that is if you want to help her." Henry nodded at Maxi.

Even though that option was closed to her, she could be a stand-in teacher of sorts.

Sabrina turned to Maxi. "What do you think? Do you want to meet me here after school for a snack and homework?"

Maxi grinned, threw her arms wide, and hugged Sabrina. "Yes! I want to be with you and not Olivia and Brooklyn!"

Olivia. Henry's girlfriend. Again. *Boy, Maxi sure doesn't like you. Or your daughter.* Both Olivia and her daughter shared the same icy blue, calculating eyes. Sabrina didn't want Maxi being cared for by that cold-calculating woman.

Henry cleared his throat, "Sometimes Olivia meets Maxi after school and takes her to my house and stays until I get home."

"That's nice," Sabrina said, although her heart skipped a beat.

Maxi folded her arms. "I don't like them."

"Why not?" Sabrina asked, leaning closer to Maxi.

"She only likes Brooklyn."

"Her daughter?" Sabrina asked. "That's how moms are."

"You treat me nice, and you're not my mom," Maxi said.

Sabrina's breath hitched in her throat at Maxi's words. When she looked up, Henry had an unreadable expression. What was he thinking?

"True, I'm not your mom," Sabrina said. But she had an invisible pull toward Maxi, one she couldn't explain. Is that what Henry was thinking, too?

Maxi continued her tirade against Olivia. "She won't help me with my homework and tells me I'm stupid. But I know I'm better at reading than Brooklyn!"

Sabrina raised her brow and turned wordlessly toward Henry. It was unacceptable to tell a child they were stupid.

"I would never tell you that," Sabrina said.

Maxi looked up and beamed at Sabrina.

Henry ran his fingers through his hair, sighed, and leaned against the table. "We should go."

Sabrina stood and placed a hand on his arm. "I'll take care of her after school."

"I'll pay you."

She would have done it for free but could use the money.

"Thanks. I wasn't sure how I'd be able to pay my

restitution to the court without a job."

"We'll think of something," he said.

Maxi threw her arms around Sabrina. "Thank you! Thank you! Now I don't have to be with that witch!"

"Maxi!" Henry gasped. "That's not a nice thing to say."

Sabrina untangled Maxi's arms from her waist. "I'll see you on Monday after school, okay?"

Henry fished in his wallet and pulled out a couple twenties. "This should cover snacks for a couple of days."

That would cover snacks for the month, she figured. She crumbled the bills in her hand and sank back in her chair.

"So, it's all settled then?" Henry asked.

"Yes, I'll be with Maxi after school to help with homework." She turned to Maxi. "Meet me here on Monday?"

Maxi clapped her hands. "Yeah!"

Henry put his hand on Maxi's shoulder as they left the library.

Sabrina would see Maxi daily, and Maxi wouldn't be subjected to Olivia's meanness. How could Henry date a person like that? Sure, the woman was beautiful but...

She chewed her bottom lip and sighed, wishing Henry was dating her, not Olivia.

Chapter 16

Sabrina needed some new jeans; her old ones were tight and had gotten stained with yellow from a malfunctioning mustard bottle. She knew there was a thrift shop run by a local church society nearby.

She went into the thrift store to look at some clothing. When she opened the door, a tinkle of a bell heralded her entrance and someone called, "Hello! Welcome!"

After perusing the jeans, she selected three pairs to try on. They ended up fitting fine and didn't have rips or stains. She'd get them.

She tucked them under her arm and walked to the blouses. The kids' section was the next rack over and she found herself mentally wondering if Maxi would like any of the dresses they were selling.

Sabrina abandoned the shirt she had admired when she spotted a pink dress with sparkles. Would Maxi like that dress? After all, she wore a hat with sparkles to the park.

Sabrina pulled out the dress and laid it over the rack for a better look. The dress was practically brand new and the arms and pockets were covered with pink sparkles. She looked at the size—a six. Was Maxi a six? She thought so.

She envisioned Maxi twirling around in the dress. It was only three dollars… On impulse, she added it to the jeans and went to the cash register. On the counter was a basket with heart and rainbow stickers. Would Maxi like these during their tutoring sessions? Sabrina placed the stickers on top of the jeans and dress.

She plunked down the cash and left with her purchases. She couldn't wait to see Maxi's face when she saw the dress and stickers. She spent the weekend cleaning the apartment, reading, and thinking about Maxi and Henry.

Chapter 17

Sabrina's last day of work was Sunday, and she said goodbye to her co-workers. She didn't even know their names, only their badges—occasionally, they sat at the same lunch table and talked about work or the weather conditions. Had she kept herself apart from them because the job was temporary? Or because she didn't want to explain why she was a felon? She didn't know and she guessed it didn't matter.

On Monday, she visited Becki, her parole officer, and explained her layoff.

Becki responded, "Yes, I've heard from several of my people. Are you applying for other jobs?"

"I have an after-school tutoring gig with a little girl. Her father's paying me."

Becki let out a long sigh. Sabrina could imagine her job was thankless at times like these. "Enough for your restitution amount?"

"No." She wasn't sure what Henry would pay her. They hadn't talked about money exactly—but she sincerely doubted it would be enough to pay rent and restitution and eat.

"Let me talk to the court and see what I can do to get it reduced. But it will be temporary, and you will still have to pay the money. Job or no job."

"What if I moved to Detroit with my parents?"

Becki paused. "That's a little more complicated."

Wasn't everything? Sabrina watched as Becki moved a stack of papers around on her desk as if trying to decide what to do with them. Finally, Becki picked up a pen and tapped on the desk.

"We'd need to transfer you to a parole officer there if they have any openings. You'd need to stay put until we can arrange it for you."

Sabrina let out a low, drawn-out sigh. It sounded complicated. "I'll probably just stay here," she said.

"Let me know if you change your mind."

Truthfully, she didn't want to live with her parents. They were caustic at best and probably contributed to her unhappiness and using drugs. In counseling, they had discussed the need to break away from the bad influences. As much as she hated to admit it, her parents weren't good influences.

On Monday afternoon, Sabrina met Maxi after school at the library. Maxi bounded over with a big smile and greeted Sabrina with a hug.

"How was school?" Sabrina asked when Maxi sat down and put her school pack on the table.

"We're having a concert!"

Sabrina raised her brows. "Really?"

"Will you come?"

"If I can," Sabrina answered.

"You better!" Maxi said in mock seriousness. Her mouth was a thin line, but her eyes were mischievous and bright.

They worked on homework, and when Maxi completed the assignments, Sabrina put a pink heart sticker at the top of the page. Maxi grinned each time Sabrina put a sticker on her paper.

"I love heart stickers!" Maxi said, flattening a

crinkled edge of her paper. "How did you know?"

Lucky guess. Sabrina smirked. "I saw them and thought of you." She made a mental note to buy more stickers for Maxi's work. "I remembered you liked pink."

They ate snacks until it was time for Henry to pick her up.

Henry patted Sabrina's shoulder. "You have no idea how happy this makes Maxi." His fingers lingered on her shoulder a bit longer. She felt a little zing—static electricity?

He had no idea what it meant to her, either.

The after-school arrangement seemed to work well. Henry even paid her enough to cover her restitution. In essence, he was paying himself for her services. Sabrina didn't care; she loved spending time with Maxi and imagined this was what having a daughter was like, with the bonus of getting to know Henry.

At their next work session, Sabrina pulled out the dress with sparkles from her pack and handed it to Maxi.

"I saw this dress and thought of you."

Maxi's mouth opened in an "O," and Sabrina noticed the glint in her eyes.

"I love it!" Maxi grabbed it and crushed it to her chest. "I want to wear it to school!"

"Is it the right size?"

Maxi glanced at the label and nodded.

"It's yours then!"

"I can't wait to show Daddy!" Maxi smoothed out the dress, and folding it carefully, she placed it into her backpack.

At their next session, Henry called, explaining he

was still at the hospital. While she listened, her eyes went to the wall clock. It was ten to six, almost closing time.

"Would you take Maxi to get something to eat? Like, to the Moonglow?"

"Sure."

"She likes mac 'n' cheese and chicken fingers. Oh, and order me a grilled cheese. And get yourself something, too."

After the bland and often repetitious meals of ramen or cereal, a restaurant meal sounded good.

Sabrina packed up their books and papers when the lights blinked for the library closure. Hand in hand, they walked to the Moonglow.

"I love the Moonglow!" Maxi said, tipping her head back as if studying the cloudy sky. "Have you been there?"

"Lots of times," Sabrina replied automatically. She faltered and stumbled on a loose rock on the sidewalk. Wait, she thought. Was that true? Had she been to the Moonglow many times?

She remembered the inside of the restaurant—a place that had been around since…since… her parents were in high school. That couldn't be right. They were from Detroit, not Clearwater.

"Sabrina!" Maxi tugged on her sleeve. "You walked past the Moonglow!"

Sabrina shook away her convoluted thoughts, glanced around, and smiled at Maxi. "I guess I did!"

"Were you thinking about something?"

"Yes, I was, Pet."

The endearment just popped out.

"Is it okay if I call you Pet?" She remembered

Maxi saying she didn't like when Olivia called her "honey."

Maxi grinned.

They retraced their steps and headed to the restaurant door with the design of the moon etched on the window. "I guess I was thinking of something else," Sabrina said, remembering dinner before dances at this restaurant. It was casual in the front part, but more formal in the back—something for everyone, families included.

"Grandma does that all the time."

They went inside and were seated at a table by the window up front. The place wasn't too busy. It was busiest on the weekends and Friday night happy hour. The smells were the same: candle wax from the table centerpieces, meat cooking, and the tang of tomato sauce. The lights were low, and soft music played in the background. But how did she remember those things? Her mind was like a vast repository of colliding thoughts. She remembered the ambiance of the Moonglow, but she didn't—a very peculiar, confusing knowing.

The waiter brought over menus and water.

"We'll have another person joining us," Sabrina said, patting the tabletop between them.

"Daddy?" Maxi looked up.

"Yes, he wants grilled cheese." Then she remembered he liked ranch with his fries. "Does he like ranch with his fries?"

Maxi nodded. "It's disgusting."

Sabrina laughed. "So, you've tried it?"

Maxi again nodded knowingly. "Catsup is better."

Sabrina would have to agree with Maxi in that

respect. She studied the menu while the waiter stood patiently. "Do you know what you want?"

Maxi said, "Macaroni and cheese, please. And chicken fingers and chocolate milk!"

"And you?" He turned to Sabrina.

"Let me look at the menu. I don't know what I want."

"I thought you've been here before?" Maxi asked.

"I have, but I can't remember the menu choices." Sabrina flipped the pages. "Give me a sec."

Sabrina's mind raced as she perused the menu. She was sure she had been here before, but couldn't remember the menu—her eyes moved over the salads. She'd have the chef's salad. She looked up and smiled at Maxi, who was watching her intently.

Sabrina waved to the waiter that she was ready. "Is this a new menu?"

He frowned. "I've worked here for three years, and it's been the same."

She had been in prison, so the menu change might have happened then. "Hmm," Sabrina hummed. "Well, I'll have the chef salad." She handed him her menu and he backed away, still writing on his tablet.

The door opened, and a bell sounded. Henry.

The wind had blown his hair, and it stood up. He looked around the room until he spotted them.

A man from the back called, "Hello, Dr. Comstock!"

Henry turned to the man. "Fred!" he called out. "How's your leg?"

"Just fine, doc." Fred got up, walked to where Henry stood, and shook hands. "Thanks to you." Fred looked over to Maxi and Sabrina. "Your family?"

"Yes." Henry slid in next to Maxi.

Sabrina smiled, and Maxi grinned.

"Well, I'll let you enjoy the fam." Fred went back to his table.

Henry waved him off. He looked tired with the crease on his forehead, making his scar more pronounced. His eyes were red-rimmed with fatigue. He smoothed back his messy hair.

Sabrina longed to run her fingers over his forehead and smooth out the crease. "What happened?" Sabrina asked, leaning forward. "Long day?"

"A bus accident involving the boys' basketball team. We must have had every one of them in the ER for scrapes, bruises, and a couple of broken bones." Henry rubbed his eyes.

"Oh, my goodness, but no one was seriously injured?"

"The bus driver has a concussion."

"Daddy!" Maxi interrupted. "What happened? What's a concussion?"

He sipped his water, and it seemed to revive him somewhat. "A concussion is when someone is hit on the head and they are dizzy and disoriented."

Maxi nodded like she understood.

"What happened exactly?" Sabrina asked.

"A tractor-trailer pulled out in front of the bus, and they T-boned the side."

"That's funny," Maxi said.

Henry turned to Maxi. "It wasn't funny."

Her face sobered. "You said T-boned!"

"Oh." Henry gave her a small smile. "It is a funny term," he agreed.

Sabrina motioned for Maxi to look at her and

demonstrated with her hands what a T-bone looked like. "This hand is the bus, and this one is the truck."

"I get it!" Maxi said.

Their food arrived, and they were silent as they ate. Sabrina watched Henry dunk his fries in the ranch dressing. Maxi wrinkled her nose.

"What?" Henry asked, noticing their interest.

"That's gross, Daddy."

Henry looked at both of them. "Neither of you likes ranch with fries?" In unison, they shook their heads. "Suit yourself."

It was cozy eating like this. The warehouse cafeteria had been noisy and chaotic and eating dinner at home was quiet and, frankly, lonely—this was the perfect combo of both and felt friendly.

Sabrina surveyed the room. Several tables held families, she guessed, eating and enjoying each other's company—like what they were doing. This feeling of togetherness was something she had never experienced with her parents. Dinner, if even prepared, was haphazard and tense. Then another family popped into her brain—parents who adored their daughter and relished their time together.

She turned her attention to the salad and noticed Henry watching her. She wiped her mouth and hoped she didn't have something stuck to her face or teeth.

"I need to thank you for helping with Maxi." Henry picked up a fry. "All she talks about at home is Sabrina this and Sabrina that. She loves the stickers you use. I'm a little jealous she has you and not me," he said, putting the fry in the ranch before popping it in his mouth with a grin.

"She loves you very much." Sabrina looked over as

Maxi swallowed a bite of her mac and cheese. "Don't you, Pet?"

Maxi nodded, licking the cheese from her lips.

Henry smiled. "Pet. I like that."

"She talks about her daddy all the time," Sabrina said.

"I'm glad she has you because of my long hours."

"What about your girlfriend?" Sabrina asked.

Henry suddenly became interested in his half-eaten sandwich.

Maxi wrinkled her nose. "I don't like Olivia." Her fork clanked on the empty plate. "She calls me Honey." Maxi's eyes glinted darkly, and she shook her head. "Honey is for bees. And bees sting!"

The black cloud of Olivia seemed to hang over them until Henry shrugged and turned to Sabrina. "Maxi doesn't like any of the women I bring home."

Sabrina raised her brows.

"I'm not sure what to do." Henry wiped his mouth and threw his napkin down.

Maxi stared at her father. "I like Sabrina. Date her!" Maxi folded her arms.

Out of the mouths of babes comes the truth.

Henry smiled at his daughter and then at Sabrina and tipped his head.

Was that a question she saw in his eyes? Or was she just wishful thinking? The very thought made her heart speed up.

Chapter 18

Now that she wasn't working, her days consisted of applying for online jobs, reading, walking, and waiting for Maxi to leave school. She still saw Becki on Thursdays and met with her parole support group in the library basement. But the lack of activities bored her— the high point of her day was seeing Maxi. She still helped with GED tutoring when needed, but that was hit or miss. She needed more to do.

Perhaps the bakery down the street would let her help in the kitchen to improve her baking skills? She'd wash dishes, anything to fill her empty hours!

"How's the job search going?" Becki asked.

Sabrina sat in the chair by Becki's massive wooden desk, which took up most of the tiny office.

"It's going," she said, stifling a yawn.

"You don't sound very enthused. Nothing out there?"

"I'm thinking of going to the bakery and see if they'd let me wash dishes, anything to keep me busy."

Becki raised her brows and pushed back her unruly hair with a hand topped with tattoos. "Do they have a paying position?" Becki asked.

"I don't know." Sabrina slumped down. "Tutoring pays pretty good." Henry was generous, paying her almost ten dollars an hour more than the warehouse. That and the small unemployment check kept her from going under. She figured she could scrape by and keep the apartment if she ate ramen most nights.

"Keep looking," Becki advised. Their meeting was officially over when Becki glanced at her watch.

Sabrina trudged over to the library to wait for the support group. She checked out three more books and began to read one of them as she waited. The library had a few comfortable chairs around the perimeter for patrons. She snagged one.

"Hey!" Billy said. "You're early."

She looked up from her book and smiled. "You too."

"This is my last session."

"Oh?"

"I'm officially off parole next week. And I got called back to the warehouse."

"You're lucky," she said, using her finger as a placeholder for her book.

He slumped into the chair next to her. "What about you?"

"I haven't been called back but have a three-hour-after-school tutoring/babysitting job."

"That's something."

"Yes." She kneaded her thigh as she talked to Billy. Yes, she was fortunate Henry had offered her some monetary help.

"So…" Billy whistled. "I might not see you again."

"I wish you luck," Sabrina said.

"And…"

Sabrina looked up as a shadow fell over them. Olivia.

"Hi." Olivia arched her brows at Sabrina. "Savannah, right?"

"Sabrina."

"Oh, yes, I remember." She pretended to slap her forehead. "A weird name."

Sabrina frowned. Her comment didn't dignify a response.

Olivia continued, "I don't mean to interrupt you and your boyfriend," Olivia said, arching an eyebrow, taking in Billy's appearance—faded jeans, worn sneakers, and sweatshirt. She stuck out her hand. "I'm Olivia."

"Billy," he said. "We're just friends." He nodded toward Sabrina.

"Right!" Olivia said, her smile got bigger. "I'm Henry's fiancée." She emphasized fiancée, although Sabrina didn't see a ring. "I mean," she said, looking down at her bare finger. "That's the next step for us."

Billy leaned forward, his elbows on his knees. "Who's Henry?" He turned to Sabrina. "Is he in our group?"

"Alison's husband."

"Ah!"

"Group?" Olivia asked, a frown creasing her brow.

"Yes, a support group," Sabrina answered, although she didn't want to reveal more to Olivia and hoped Billy wouldn't either.

"Like AA?"

"Something like that," Sabrina said softly.

"Congrats on your engagement," Billy said, using his hands on his thighs to stand.

"Thank you!" Olivia said, her face glowing at the thought of marrying Henry. "Anyway, when we get married, we won't need your help." She looked pointedly at Sabrina.

"Sure."

Olivia did a little shuffle with her feet. "I'm going to get Brookie for gymnastics, but I thought I'd drop off these books."

Sabrina bet she was a cheerleader in school by the way she bounced on her toes. Olivia's forehead never moved when she smiled. Did she use injectables? And her makeup cracked and looked blotchy and her lipstick had bled into the fine lines around her mouth. On further inspection, Sabrina guessed Olivia's beauty came from a tube or bottle.

"She seems nice," Billy said as Olivia skipped away.

Sabrina did a one-shoulder shrug. *So do grizzly bears until they're provoked.* She rolled her eyes. "I guess," she said.

Billy laughed. "It's obvious she's bothered by you."

"Why?"

"Have you looked at yourself in the mirror lately?"

"No."

"You're a beautiful woman!" Billy nudged her shoulder. "In a natural way. You don't need all that goop on your face like she does."

Sabrina waved a hand, dismissing him. "I don't look at myself in the mirror. All I see is the face of a girl who made bad choices and now doesn't have many options. I don't think I'm anything special."

"You're wrong."

She didn't want to talk about looks so she changed the subject. "Tell me more about Alison."

"I remember something else my aunt shared about Alison.

Sabrina leaned forward expectantly.

"She was a teacher."

Sabrina knew that from the newspaper reports about the accident, and Henry had also told her about his wife's profession.

"She fell apart after her husband was killed and began to teach adult education," Billy continued.

Sabrina had seen Alison's adult education picture in the yearbook.

"I know. I couldn't face the kids in the main part of the school. The place we met. Rob and I."

Billy looked at her with a curious expression. "You said 'you couldn't.' "

The thoughts that ran through her mind made it seem like she was the one with the nervous breakdown. It certainly felt that way.

"I did?"

"Yes, you said, 'I couldn't face the kids.' " He chuckled. "It was almost like you were Alison in a way."

"There's no way that could happen."

"It's possible," Billy said. "You know."

"What is?" Sabrina asked. Billy seemed to be speaking in riddles today.

"People switching places."

Sabrina frowned at him.

"Like they switched jobs or families?" She remembered a television program like that, or maybe it was a movie?

"No, I have a friend who switched souls when he tried to commit suicide."

"Really?" Sabrina leaned forward, assessing Billy's sincerity. Nothing about his person revealed he was telling her a tale.

He continued, "Both parties have to agree to switch."

Could you even see a person's soul? she wondered. "People can switch souls?" She couldn't wrap her mind around the concept.

Then, a vague and unclear memory of a glittering and misty place. A place she had gone after the car accident. There was a girl, a woman, but she couldn't remember what happened.

"Yes, he called it a 'walk-in soul,' " Billy said. He frowned like he was trying to remember all the details.

Her mind continued whirling. Who would she have switched with? The idea was intriguing and a bit frightening.

Sabrina swallowed thickly before asking, "Did he say who he switched with?"

"No, but he began to lead a different life. He was pretty depressed before and tried to shoot himself."

She had been depressed before the accident, too, but did she want to switch her life with someone else? The whole concept seemed pretty far-fetched.

"There are books about it, I think," Billy said, glancing at the clock. "We better go. The group starts in ten minutes." They followed several other attendees down the stairs to the meeting room in the basement.

After everyone was seated and the new parolees were introduced, the leader, Charlie Daniels's look-alike, said, "First, let's hear some good news."

Sabrina zoned out. Her mind was on what Billy had shared with her—a walk-in soul. All through group, she half listened to the talk around her, the other half on "walk-in souls" and the consequences it would entail.

She led a very different life before the accident and was now a more—*what's the word?*—*respectable* person…but had attributed it to growing up and getting clean in prison.

Did she switch with Alison Comstock? That would explain the memories—her feelings for Maxi and Henry. The pieces were falling into place. Sabrina was certain she had Alison's soul in her body. It was spooky yet intriguing.

Billy raised his hand. "I'm off parole next week, and I've been hired in receiving at the warehouse permanently."

"Let's give Billy a round of applause!"

They did, and she clapped along. Sabrina was genuinely glad for him. She had another year to go until she was off parole.

"Anyone else have something positive to share?"

A woman named Cheryl piped up. "I got my driver's license back! It's been five years."

They clapped for Cheryl.

"I got a job," another said.

More applause.

Sabrina thought to herself—she had a new soul, but she needed a new job.

Chuck gazed at their group and when no one said more, he began, "Okay, let's talk about the challenges of being on parole."

She knew she needed to participate somehow, so she raised her hand. "Limited job choices." Her mouth said the words, but her mind was still on Alison's soul.

She also wanted to ask the group if they knew about walk-in souls but thought better.

"Anyone else feel the same way?"

Sabrina looked at the people who circled Chuck, and most were nodding.

"What are some jobs you can have with a prison record?" Chuck asked.

"My brother-in-law is a plumber," someone volunteered.

"I know a guy who works in a construction office."

The suggestions continued.

When the meeting finished, she hugged Billy and wished him luck. He said, "Check out the walk-in soul idea."

Chapter 19

Billy's suggestion about having a walk-in soul stuck with her. She had purposefully gotten to the library early to search for answers. Sabrina asked the librarian to show her where the new-age books were located and found three with small sections about walk-in souls. She checked them out and stowed them in her pack to read tonight.

When Maxi arrived, Sabrina tried to concentrate on Maxi's homework and the way she stuck out her tongue as she worked. But "walk-in souls" kept pushing to the forefront and was all she could think about.

If it was Alison with whom she had switched places, that would account for the feelings she had for Maxi and Henry. She was the logical person. That would explain the memories that were real but seemed shrouded in a layer of gauze. She could see them through the haze of her mind. And her feelings for Maxi? Her breath stuck in her throat. She had feelings for Maxi because she was her mother. And Henry…? What would he think if she told him she had become his dead wife? She swallowed. Would he let her keep seeing Maxi? Or think she was crazy and keep Maxi away from her?

After she and Maxi did homework and ate snacks, they began reading *Anne of Green Gables* together—a favorite when Sabrina was little. No, correct that statement; the book was Alison's favorite.

Henry arrived fifteen minutes early as they were still reading, their heads bent close to avoid bothering the other nearby patrons.

"Hi!"

His voice in the quiet library caused Sabrina to jump.

"Sorry, I startled you."

"Daddy!" Maxi smiled at him. "We're reading a book together. One of Sabrina's favorites!"

"And what is that?"

"*Anne of Green Gables.*"

"Your mother liked that book too."

"She did?" Maxi scrunched up her face. "I wish she was here."

Sabrina sat on her hands and willed herself not to say anything to Henry until the right time and she was sure. How does one become sure about something like that exactly? Perhaps the books she checked out would help.

"Me too," he said. He pulled up a straight-backed chair from a nearby table. "I have a favor to ask Sabrina."

She felt her brows raise in anticipation.

"I have a meeting Saturday morning at work and was wondering if you'd watch Maxi at the park until I finished?"

"I'd love to!"

"Good. I was going to ask Olivia, but there seems to be a conflict between Maxi and Brooklyn. And my mother's sick."

"I'd be happy to spend the morning with Maxi. We always have a good time together."

"I don't like Brooklyn or Olivia!" Maxi said, her mouth in a pout and her arms folded defensively across her chest.

"Don't worry, Pet," Sabrina said, wiping a stray strand of hair from Maxi's cheek. "We can read and play games or just play in the park if you like."

"I'm glad Grandma can't babysit."

"But you like your grandmother, don't you?" Sabrina asked. "Grandmas are special people."

Maxi wrinkled her nose. "She makes me learn to knit."

Sabrina hid a smile. Knitting didn't sound like a lot of fun to her either.

Maxi's expression changed to happiness. "But we also make cookies!"

"There! You see!"

"I guess I like being with Grandma, but I like you too."

"Thank you, Pet, for that vote of confidence."

She looked up, and Henry stared intently at her. What was he thinking? Did he feel the connection, too? When he accidentally brushed her sleeve, she felt a shock. That was just static electricity and nothing else, but still…She gave him a weak smile. "I'll see you tomorrow and Saturday."

"Thank you. I don't know what I'd do without you," he said. He reached out his hand, took her fingers in his, and gently squeezed.

Chapter 20

Later, after Henry and Maxi left the library, Sabrina returned to the apartment and fixed herself a cup of ramen noodles and an orange. She sat down to eat and read one of the books she had checked out that mentioned walk-in souls.

She ran her finger down the table of contents, which had only two pages written about the concept. Some people believed it was possible for the original soul of a person to leave one body and for another soul to "walk in." She chewed her lip as she read. Why wasn't this stuff well-known?

She wanted to talk to Billy further but didn't know how to reach him. She sipped her soup as she contemplated this new information. She couldn't talk to Maxi or Henry about this. She didn't know any of the other women in the group well. No, she needed to figure this out herself.

She reread the paragraph about the walk-in soul and how the exchange was made. The ingredients were two people, but one wanted to leave this life. The other person needed to agree to take their soul so their spirit could live on.

She and Alison?

Sabrina thought about this new phenomenon. She wasn't sure of the mechanics. Did something else happen before the soul switch? And what happened to the other soul? Did they have to go into the depressed person's body? She had more questions and wished Billy had shared more, but he was vague on the particulars.

She picked up the next book and ran her finger down the list of topics, searching for the section on walk-in souls. This one quoted someone named Montgomery about her beliefs. She had written several books on the subject. Did the library have those for checkout?

****

When Saturday rolled around, she was happy to go to the park with Maxi and enjoy the fresh air without stressing over walk-ins. Henry would drop Maxi off at nine, and they would meet at the swings. Sabrina put some snacks in her pack in case Maxi got hungry.

As usual, Maxi bounded out of Henry's car and ran toward Sabrina with her arms outstretched. They collided and wrapped their arms around each other.

"I've missed you!"

Maxi giggled. "You saw me last night."

"I know!" Sabrina reached out to pick her up, and they shared a hug. "I've missed you since then."

"Wow!" Henry said, pushing his hand through his hair. "I don't get that kind of reception from Maxi!"

"Oh, Daddy!" Maxi said, leaning over in Sabrina's arms. "Come here!" Maxi tugged his arm to join in the hug.

Sabrina felt his arms around them and was close enough to get a whiff of his aftershave—woodsy and fresh. She needed to pull herself away from the unsettling thoughts of the handsome doctor.

"That's better," he said, his arms stretched out,

looking into Sabrina's eyes. "I'm getting jealous of how she talks about you all the time."

Sabrina laughed. "And when I see her, she talks about you!"

"Oh, good. I was getting worried," he said in a mock-stern voice. "I better get to my meeting." He squeezed them both.

She wondered what he saw in her eyes. He seemed to be searching for some kind of answer, but she didn't know his question.

"Later!" Henry untangled himself and waved as he ran to his car.

"What do you want to do first?" she asked Maxi, putting her down, taking her hand, and swinging their joined arms.

"The slide." Maxi took off running.

It was always the slide.

Several hours passed while they played on all the equipment.

"Sabrina?"

"Yes, Pet?"

Sabrina slumped into the swing. She was out of shape and panted when they finished climbing on the jungle gym.

"Can you teach me how to do a cartwheel?"

"Sure, why?"

"Brooklyn can do one, and she's teaching some girls a cheer. Because I can't do a cartwheel, she won't let me join them."

Sabrina felt her internal temperature rise and her cheeks flush—*Brooklyn and Olivia.* She was beginning to understand why Maxi disliked them. What did Henry see in Olivia besides she was gorgeous?

Even with Sabrina's lack of experience with dating, she knew there had to be more than just a handsome or pretty face. There had to be common ground. Olivia didn't seem to even like Maxi.

"Do you want to do it here?" The grass was wet from the dew, and the cement area had tables and chairs. Where would the best place be to do a cartwheel?

Maxi touched the grass and wrinkled her nose. "It's wet."

They stood on the sidewalk. Did she remember how to do a cartwheel? A memory of a girl in a short, pleated skirt doing a back flip raced through her mind.

"If I remember…" Sabrina tapped her chin. "I think it goes like this." She placed one foot in front of the other and arched her body, her arms taking her weight as she swung her legs up and over. She dusted off her hands when finished. "How was that?"

"Pretty good," Maxi said, nodding enthusiastically.

"Do you want to try?" Sabrina asked. She'd stand by Maxi and guide her legs over. Maxi placed her legs in the position and leaned over so her hands met the cement, and Sabrina helped her legs up and over.

"I did it!" Maxi shook her arms up.

They heard a bell—someone on a bicycle was barreling toward them, and they jumped aside.

"Maybe this isn't a good place to practice," Sabrina said, holding Maxi against her as a line of bicycles flowed past.

"Maybe you can come to our house?" Maxi asked. "We have a big backyard."

"Possibly." Would Henry want her there?

"We live close," Maxi said, looking around and

nodding.

Sabrina scanned for more bicyclists, and when the coast was clear, they continued doing cartwheels. After about half an hour, Sabrina slumped against a nearby tree. "I'm beat."

Maxi hugged her. "Thank you for helping me. I'll practice."

"Good."

They returned to sit on the swings.

When Henry returned, Maxi said, "Sabrina's helping me learn to do cartwheels!"

He studied Maxi and then Sabrina. "She is?"

He had an unreadable expression, and Sabrina wanted to know what he was thinking.

"She was a cheerleader!" Maxi said.

That remark made Sabrina stop. Had she been a cheerleader? She had vague memories of wearing a uniform, jumping up and down, and clapping her hands while chanting, "Go, team! Go!"

"You were?" he asked.

Momentarily, her brain froze on the images. "Uh, was I? What?"

"A cheerleader," he prompted.

"I guess I was."

He tilted his head, studying her. She couldn't imagine what he thought of her—inconsistent answers and not remembering details of her life, but perhaps he attributed it to head trauma left over from the accident.

"Can she come to our house to practice?" Maxi jerked on his coat.

"I don't see why not." He cleared his throat. "I have a better idea for now. Can we take you to dinner?"

Dinner would be a nice switch from ramen noodles

and boxed mac and cheese. "I'd like that."

"Are you free tonight?"

"Yes." She was free most nights.

"I'd like to thank you for your help with Maxi."

"But you already paid me."

"Maxi is priceless to me."

Sabrina nodded. "I understand. I love her too."

He moved his hand toward her, and she automatically reached for it. Her response surprised her, yet it didn't. He squeezed her fingers. "I can tell you do." He continued holding her hand, giving it light pressure. "I'll pick you up at five?" She felt the zing of electricity between them.

"The Heritage Apartments."

"And don't forget," Maxi said, "about my concert!" She shook her finger at Sabrina.

"I won't, Pet. I won't."

Henry held her hand until he gently untangled their fingers and entered the car.

Sabrina continued to watch the car with 4EAEA license plates drive away. Suddenly, she knew what 4EAEA meant—Forever and Ever, Always. She rubbed her fingers, the one with the electricity against her jeans. There was a connection between them, but she didn't know exactly what it meant.

Chapter 21

Sabrina stood on the sidewalk, her mouth agape, and closed it as kids on skateboards raced past her. *Dinner,* she internally shrieked. They were taking her to dinner! She looked down at her stained jeans, black, scuffed work boots, and oversized sweatshirt. She'd have plenty of time to go to the thrift store and find something nice to wear—maybe a pretty new blouse.

She hurried toward the thrift store and hoped they were still open. There, she looked through the blouses, selected several in her size, and tried them on. She favored the turquoise one with lace at the sleeves. By the cash register was a display of barrettes and some hair clips. She found one with some fake green stones that would look nice with her hair and blouse.

She secured everything in her pack and hurried home for a quick shower. Then, she applied some lip gloss and eyeshadow she had found in the drawer. When she looked in the mirror, a different girl smiled back.

Yes, she looked pretty this way and hoped Maxi and Henry would notice, too. She was nervous and wiped her sweaty palms on her jeans.

He arrived in his silver-gray sedan and opened the door for her. She peered into the back seat. "Where's Maxi?"

"Change of plans. A sleepover with some girls in

her class, and she wanted to go. It's just me. Hope that's okay."

"Of course! I get that dinner isn't very exciting for a seven-year-old."

She fastened her seatbelt.

"You look nice," Henry said as he took the car out of park, and they drove away.

"Where are we going?" she asked, suddenly feeling shy. They were alone in a confined space. She had wanted to be alone with Henry, but now that they were together, she didn't know how to behave.

She stayed quiet and watched the scenery flash by.

"I thought we might drive to Holland to a new restaurant one of my patients told me about." He turned briefly so their eyes met.

His were fathomless brown pools, and hers were now rimmed with charcoal liner and a soft taupe shadow—forgotten makeup her mother must have left behind.

They drove through areas Sabrina wasn't familiar with, taking the coastline of Lake Michigan. The harbors were filled with sailboats, motorboats, and houseboats. "This is nice." She couldn't imagine what it would feel like to be on a boat moving in the water.

"I like this drive." Henry gripped the steering wheel. "It helps clear my head."

She could only imagine what his job was like.

"Tell me about your work," she said, turning slightly in her seat to face him. So much for feeling shy and quiet.

He ran his fingers through his hair, making the front stick up, but it didn't distract from his good looks, even with the scar on his forehead.

"Emergency rooms are chaotic places most of the time. It's frustrating because we get people who shouldn't be there. They'd be better served at a med stop."

"For what sorts of things?"

"Colds, the flu, stomachaches. E.R.s are for people with heart attacks, broken bones, gunshots, auto accidents—serious ailments."

"I see."

"But I think my job might change, and I may need more help with Maxi. So, I'm glad she's at a sleepover." He flicked his eyes to her. "We can talk without her putting in her two cents."

Sabrina smiled inwardly, imagining Maxi's bright smile and upturned nose telling her father what she wanted and didn't. There was nothing shy about her.

Since she had nothing better to do than care for Maxi, she raised her brows, an invitation to continue.

"I'll explain over dinner," he said.

She nodded and turned back to watch Lake Michigan on one side and tall, stately pine trees and big houses on the other. Could she even imagine living in such a place? Some of the houses looked the same size as her entire apartment building.

Henry seemed to know where he was going, and they pulled into a parking lot for a restaurant aptly named Jack's on the Lake.

They went in, and Henry told the hostess, "We're early. We have reservations." He gave her the details.

The hostess looked around. "We'll have a table for you in about fifteen minutes."

"We'll wait in the bar."

He put his hand on the small of her back and

guided her into the bar, and they snagged a high table overlooking the boats. Sabrina noticed several heads turn in their direction.

She felt self-conscious and smoothed down the blouse. "Am I dressed for this place?"

"Yes, why?"

"I see people staring at me."

He chuckled. "You're beautiful, Sabrina."

"I am?"

"Yes."

She felt her cheeks flush. He thought she was beautiful. No one had ever told her that before, and her heart skipped a beat. She ducked her head and willed her heart to slow down and concentrate on the drinks menu.

"I'm sorry if I embarrassed you," he said.

"I'm not used to compliments."

"Do you know what you want?"

She had no idea what to order, so she turned to look out the window. "I love the view!"

"What can I get you?" he asked.

"I don't usually drink." She chewed her lip. "I'm not supposed to drink while on parole."

Henry cocked his head. "How about a Shirley Temple?"

"What's that?"

"A drink without the alcohol. One of Maxi's favorites."

"That sounds perfect."

Henry left and returned with a beer for him and the soda with cherries for her. She took a tiny sip of her drink. She liked it. "This is good."

"I'm glad."

"And you?" She nodded toward his glass.

"An IPA they make here."

She had never heard of an IPA before. Her dad drank the cheapest beer he could find.

"What does IPA mean?"

"India pale ale. A term from when Britain ruled India. It was the beer they made there."

"Oh! I just keep learning all sorts of new things." Her voice rose steadily. Several heads swiveled in her direction, and she cleared her throat.

"Like what?" Henry asked before taking a long drink from his beer.

"You'll think this is strange, but a man in my counseling group told me about someone who had switched souls. That seems pretty far-fetched, doesn't it?"

Suddenly, she wished she hadn't confessed something so out there with Henry. Would he think she was a nut?

Henry kept watching her, his head tilted to one side. He wasn't laughing; he was only studying her, which made her uncomfortable. Did he think she was insane?

"I don't think that's strange at all," he finally said before taking a drink and continuing to watch her over his raised glass.

"You don't?" She ran her fingers down the edge of the glass, leaving streaks.

"No."

Henry's name was called for their table. She hoped they could continue talking about switched souls. They took their drinks and followed the hostess to a table covered with a white cloth and flowers.

"I understand fish is their specialty," Henry said.

She liked fish, she guessed—fish sticks, in particular, or tuna fish.

"You'll need to let me know the best kind of fish to order."

"Perch or salmon from Lake Michigan," he said, not looking up from the menu. "My favorite's perch."

Maybe she'd try perch, too.

While they waited for their meals, Henry cleared his throat. "I've been offered a new job, which means a longer commute. Currently, my mother comes over and helps in the morning, but she's working again, and it's not always possible for her to come over. I'm looking to hire someone to move in and be a nanny/helper/housekeeper/chef for Maxi…" He paused. "And me."

"Oh! What about when you and Olivia get married?" Sabrina asked.

"Whatever gave you the idea I was going to marry her?" he asked, his eyes narrowed.

"Olivia said you were engaged."

"We're not." His words made it quite clear they weren't engaged.

"Oh?" She picked up her glass and sipped, the bubbles seemed to fizz around her nose.

"The woman I marry must have Maxi's approval, and Olivia doesn't have it, I'm afraid."

"So you'd hire me to live with you and Maxi and help care for her?"

"And me," he said.

"Oh!"

"Make some meals, get Maxi to and from school, homework help, maybe do some laundry, and keep things picked up."

"And you want me to do that?"

"If you'd like." He continued to study her.

"What does Maxi think?"

Henry chuckled. "If it involves you, she'd be up for anything. In a short time, you've completely won her over!"

Sabrina would be able to live in a real house and take care of Maxi. It sounded like a dream come true.

"I'd love to care for Maxi."

"And me," Henry added.

"And you, of course." Her gaze dropped to the table, suddenly feeling shy with him.

"Good! I was hoping you'd say yes."

She still owed him almost seventeen thousand dollars in restitution. But her acceptance had nothing to do with the money she owed him. She loved Maxi with all her heart and couldn't bear to be parted from her. Was her reaction all Sabrina or all Alison? She was beginning to try to untwist the two souls as memories crowded each other.

"We'll talk again next week to hammer out the details."

She ordered the perch and had never had such a wonderful meal before. She felt as buoyant as the boats bobbing in the water and wanted to pinch herself. She'd get to be with Maxi! And Henry, she realized. She loved him too, but in a different way. Did she love him because he gave her a second chance, or was it something else?

"Will you tell Maxi?" Sabrina asked. "Or should I let her know?"

"Yes, when she returns from her sleepover. She'll

be excited. She needs a mother figure in her life. My mother's too old and outdated in her ways. You'll be good for Maxi."

"She'll be good for me," Sabrina said, swallowing thickly. "I feel as if I can right a wrong after killing her mother." She studied her half-eaten food. "Does Maxi know who I am?"

"I shared the bare bones with her. I didn't keep it a secret."

"I wondered." She poked at her food and then took another bite. "I wasn't sure you had because Maxi is always glad to see me. I didn't know if she'd react differently if she knew I killed her mother."

"You told her about the accident when we first met. You didn't mean to kill Alison, and you served your time."

"I've changed. I'm a completely different person."

Henry tilted his head, studying her. "What were you like before?"

She searched around in the residue of her mind for an answer to his question. "It's hard for me to remember. I think I was a troubled teen who hated her parents and didn't want to move to Clearwater. I thought it was the worst idea my parents ever had. I didn't try in school and never went to class. Then I had the accident, and—poof—my life started."

"That's interesting. Something similar happened to me." He moved aside his hair to show her the scar on his forehead.

She nodded before tilting her chin and brushing back her hair so he could see the thin, almost invisible scar that sliced her cheek. "I've got one too, and others you can't see."

"Maybe someday you'll show me the others'?" he asked.

Her breath caught momentarily. "Maybe." And her mind went to the scars on her stomach and thighs. She'd be mostly naked if she showed him the rest.

Would they get to that point if she lived at his house? Would it be the casual way her parents had lounged around the living room half-dressed—a comfortable way families co-existed? She was sure Henry would see more than her scars if she let him.

Henry signaled for another beer. "My accident was somewhat different. I was the last car in a three-car pileup on a foggy night. I was the only one to survive."

"And that's where you got your scar?"

"I have others you can't see, too." His beer arrived, and he sipped the foam at the top. "So I understand a bit about what you're feeling, and I see death every day in the E.R. I may view it differently than others." He paused to take a long drink. "I loved Alison very much. I don't know why her time with me was short." Henry hung his head briefly. "I know everyone dies; it's a fact of life—whether accidental, natural, or on purpose."

Sabrina watched him. What was he trying to tell her?

"Are you trying to say you've forgiven me?"

"I'm just saying I don't know why it happened, and I don't want you to continue to beat yourself up over it. I hope you're not saying yes to moving in with us because you feel guilty."

"Nothing could be farther from the truth." Sabrina shook her head.

"Good." He wiped his mouth with the napkin.

"When I told you about walk-in souls, you weren't

surprised." She studied him as he fiddled with his knife.

"As a doctor, I've seen and experienced many things that border on the unexplained. Part of my training as a doctor is to look at the facts and symptoms. But personally, do I believe souls can switch around, you ask? My answer would be yes."

Henry's phone buzzed. He pulled it out and squinted. "I guess we need to go back. Maxi wants to come home and not stay at the sleepover. You don't mind if we leave, do you?"

"Of course not."

"We can take dessert to go if you like?"

"No, I couldn't eat another bite. It was delicious."

"Good. We'll come again."

He paid the bill before they drove to the house where the sleepover was held, and Henry went to the door and walked a sleepy, tearful Maxi to the car.

"Are you okay?" Sabrina asked after she was in her booster seat.

Maxi nodded and sniffed. "I missed Daddy."

"Her first sleepover with friends and not Grandma," Henry explained.

"It can be scary sleeping in a strange place," Sabrina said and reached back to take Maxi's hand.

"Thank you for coming with Daddy," Maxi said. "I want to go home and sleep in my bed." Maxi yawned widely before closing her eyes.

"You can just drop me off at the Heritage."

"I'm sorry we didn't get to finish our conversation."

"That's okay."

Sabrina ran up the steps to her apartment, where there was a paper taped to the door. She stopped in the hallway and looked around before stepping closer—an eviction notice. Well, Henry's job offer came at the perfect time.

Chapter 22

The following day, Sabrina studied the apartment critically—she was finally going to live in a real home! What should she pack for the move to Henry and Maxi's, and what could be left behind?

There was nothing personal or special about this apartment. It was a place to sleep and eat. There were no good memories or stories about a family that had once been there.

She'd take her clothes, pictures, and her meager selection of books, and that was about it. When it was time to go, she could leave the battered pots and pans, chipped and cracked dishes, and lopsided and scarred furniture here. Maybe the next tenant could use them or perhaps the manager would throw this stuff away.

She went to the couch, adjusted the cushion where the foam stuck out, sat and finished her surveillance. The walls were bare. She hoped Henry had some pretty landscapes hanging over the living room couch.

In her mind's eye, she pictured Henry and Maxi's home. She hadn't been there yet, but she assumed it was warm and cozy, with Maxi's shoes and boots by the front door, family photos on the mantel or tables, and shelves full of books and comfortable overstuffed furniture where they would sit and watch TV or read.

Her head was filled with images of a blue chair with a reading lamp placed by the window and bathed by the sun's glow. She didn't know where this image had come from, but it calmed her thinking she and Maxi could sit in that chair and read *Anne of Green Gables* or other tales. She wanted that blue chair and a real home. This apartment couldn't be called home by any stretch of the imagination.

She stood, smoothed down her jeans, went into the bedroom, and began putting clothing in neat piles on the bed. Then she went into the living room. There was nothing personal or special in here—ash trays and scarred furniture tops. She imagined Henry had pictures of Maxi and Alison on the tables, etc., and maybe a vase of flowers. Why didn't her parents treasure those things? She assumed she had been happy as a child, relishing going to a park like Maxi and having her parents push her on the swing while she urged them to go faster like Maxi. She had missed so much growing up, but now she'd have a chance to view childhood through Maxi's experiences.

She shook her head sadly as she went into the kitchen and opened cupboards. Only a few cups of ramen noodles, a box of mac and cheese, and a can of chicken noodle soup. Would she need those food stuffs at Henry's? She didn't think so.

She hoped she would have the life she imagined at Henry's house. Again, there was nothing personal or cozy at this place. When she finished, she had enough to fill a garbage bag. She'd be ready to move when Henry gave the nod.

She glanced around the bedroom and decided to go to the library and perhaps the park to distract herself from wanting to move immediately and begin her new life. She wore a sweatshirt, exited the apartment, and walked to the library.

It was Sunday, and people's cars clustered around the churches gracing the middle of Clearwater. She had never attended church and wondered what it was like. Then one of those memories that felt more like a dream raced through her mind—a girl wearing a white dress standing before an altar.

She stopped by the tall white building with the reddish steeple on the roof and listened to strains of music that escaped under the door, filling the sidewalk with notes of praise and joy. When the song ended, she watched the double doors open, and people flowed out to the parking lot and sidewalk. Most moved around her like a boulder in a stream, but several wished her a "blessed day." Then Olivia and Brooklyn approached.

"Why hello, Samantha!" Olivia cooed.

"Sabrina."

"Oh, right!" Olivia was not sorry she couldn't remember Sabrina's name.

"I've been meaning to talk to you," Olivia said, lowering her voice as if she didn't want anyone to hear their conversation. "It's about Henry."

Of course, it was. Everything was about Henry.

"What about him?" She was irritated at how this woman cozied up to her like they were friends. She took a small step back. Olivia's breath smelled of old coffee.

The crowd had left the sidewalk, and the three of them were alone.

"Why don't you run along to the car, Brookie, while I talk to this person," Olivia said to Brooklyn. "You can watch something on my phone." With a backward glance, Brooklyn grabbed the phone and skipped off to the car with her mother's phone.

"What did you need to tell me?" Sabrina ran her hand through her hair.

"This babysitting arrangement."

Sabrina remained silent, wondering what Olivia could say.

"Henry didn't know how to tell you, he's regretting hiring you to care for Maxi. He was just being nice."

Still, Sabrina remained silent, her mind whirling at Olivia's words. Would Henry have wanted her to live with them if he felt this way? And why hadn't he told Sabrina this himself?

"I see."

"Yes, we talked the other day and decided it best if you didn't see Maxi anymore."

Although Sabrina knew this was untrue, there was a niggle of doubt in Olivia's words. She was ninety-nine point nine percent sure Henry didn't feel this way. He hadn't said anything at dinner. There was no way he could have discussed it with Olivia unless he talked to her late last night or early this morning.

"I better speak to him." Sabrina finally found her voice.

"Oh, no!" Olivia said. "He'll know we talked. He wanted to ease into the topic."

"Then why are you telling me this?" Sabrina swallowed and leaned away, crossing her arms.

"So you could find someplace else to work."

But Sabrina loved caring for Maxi.

"Who will take care of Maxi?"

"I will," Olivia said, fluttering her lashes.

"Hmm," Sabrina said. *Maxi didn't like Olivia.*

"I'm glad we're on the same page! It's nice to have

this little woman to woman chat." Olivia patted Sabrina's arm. Olivia leaned closer, her plastic smile frozen as if they had just shared some exciting gossip. Sabrina noticed Olivia had a glob of mascara at the corner of her eye.

Sabrina doubted they would ever be on the same page or even in the same book. She understood why Maxi disliked the woman so much—she was conniving and disingenuous.

When Olivia and Brooklyn's car exited the parking lot, Sabrina turned toward the library, her original destination. Seeing Olivia had dampened her excitement about moving in with Maxi and Henry.

Chapter 23

Sabrina waited until Monday afternoon for when she would see Maxi. She had spent the day cleaning the apartment. The manager wouldn't fault her for dirty floors or countertops. The entire place smelled overwhelmingly like pine trees. Her only fault was missed rent payments, and that couldn't have been helped.

Cleaning kept her busy until she met Maxi at the library. It also gave her time to digest Olivia's revelations. Was Henry just being nice? Or did he see Sabrina's love for Maxi? He had mentioned it when they had spoken at the restaurant. Friday seemed a long time ago, not just two days. Those two days were the happiest, yet now she was filled with doubt about her future with Maxi and Henry.

She repeated their conversations in her mind, looking for clues to his feelings for her as she scoured the kitchen sink.

Henry was a complicated man, and she had just brushed the surface of what made Henry, Henry. She had never known a man quite like him. When she thought of him, her stomach tingled, and she felt sexual stirrings. She realized she wanted to see him again almost as much as Maxi. She thought she was also falling in love with Henry.

Now, she sat at a table and watched the door for

Maxi's arrival—usually with a bang and an excited squeal. Today, she came in with another little girl—their heads were close together, and they giggled, swinging their arms between them. Sabrina smiled at Maxi as they came closer.

"You brought a friend?" Sabrina asked.

"This is Charlotte." Maxi pushed the girl forward. "You know, like Charlotte's web?"

"Yes, I know." Sabrina rolled her eyes, smiling. "Hello, Charlotte."

"Charlotte has a solo, too," Maxi said. "This is Sabrina."

Solo? Sometimes, Maxi's exuberance was hard to follow. *Ah, yes, the concert. Maxi only mentioned it every time they were together.* Sabrina wouldn't miss it for the world.

Charlotte nodded but didn't comment, but her eyes were as bright as Maxi's.

"I have a solo Wednesday night, and Charlotte does, too. You'll come, right?" she asked again.

"Yes," Sabrina promised.

Sabrina helped both of them with their homework and divided the snacks equally. When they finished, Maxi looked around. "Can we sit by the stuffed animals and read?"

"Of course. Maybe I'll check out a book and join you." She cleaned up the snack mess first, throwing the wrappers and juice boxes in the trash.

When finished, she dusted off her hands and looked around. She had exhausted the library's selection of books that mentioned "walk-in souls" and selected a popular novel to read instead.

She took her book and sat by the girls. A giant

teddy bear seemed to lean into them. The girls finished their cheese crackers while reading and showing pictures to the assorted stuffed animals gathered in a circle.

Sabrina pretended to read when Charlotte whispered to Maxi, "Who's Sabrina? Is she your new mommy?"

"No, my mom's dead."

"You don't have a mommy?" Charlotte asked Maxi.

Sabrina stopped reading and waited for Maxi's answer, hiding her face behind her book.

"No, she died when I was born."

"You didn't get a new mother?"

Maxi grimaced. "My dad thought Olivia would be a good mother, but I don't like her." Maxi shook her head, making her hair fall over her eyes. She brushed it away.

"Hmm," Charlotte said, furrowing her brows. "I feel bad you don't have a mother."

Maxi shrugged. "I want a mommy like Sabrina."

In surprise, Sabrina dropped her book. "Me?" she said with a squeak.

"I love you!" Maxi said, crawling across the floor to hug Sabrina's legs.

"And I love you too, Pet." She rested her chin on Maxi's head until Maxi returned to her place by Charlotte.

"Let's fix Sabrina up with your dad," Charlotte said.

The girls froze when Henry's shadow fell over them.

"Are you talking about me?" Henry asked.

"Charlotte wants to fix you up with Sabrina." Maxi blinked innocently.

Henry stared at Sabrina but made his comments to Maxi. "You don't say…Why do you say that?"

"I love Sabrina and want her for my mommy."

"It's a bit more complicated than that," he said, breaking eye contact with Sabrina to squat down on his haunches to look at Maxi.

Maxi pouted.

"Have you asked Sabrina what she thinks?"

They all turned toward her and she couldn't hide behind her book.

"Sabrina?"

Sabrina felt her cheeks warm. "I'd love to be your mother, Maxi," she hugged Maxi, "but adults have to make that decision to be parents or even husband and wife."

Maxi frowned. "I wish it was easier!"

"I've got an idea," Henry said.

Maxi looked up at him, and her mouth opened, waiting for her father to continue.

"How about Sabrina moves in with us and helps care for you instead of Grandma?"

"Will you?" Maxi turned to Sabrina with her mouth open.

It was practically all she thought about since they had dinner. "Yes!" she practically screamed.

Would Henry ask her to move in if he didn't want her to babysit Maxi? Olivia's words didn't ring true. Olivia hoped Sabrina would disappear. She wasn't going to.

"Goody!" Maxi clapped her hands.

Charlotte picked up the book.

"Can we stay here?" Maxi asked and turned to Charlotte and the book they had been reading.

"For a bit." Henry ruffled her hair and stood up. "I want to talk to Sabrina."

Henry carried two cups from a local coffee shop. He set them down on the table, offered her a hand, and led her to the table.

"Sorry about all the mommy talk." Henry blew on his coffee before taking a sip. "I don't know why Maxi says what she says."

"I do. She wants you to be happy." Sabrina placed her hands around her coffee. "She loves you very much."

"It's awkward, though."

"She's just being honest," Sabrina said.

"Sorry to saddle you with Charlotte, too."

"She's a sweet girl—nicer than Brooklyn."

Henry made a noise deep in his throat at the mention of Brooklyn.

She sipped companionably. Henry did, too, and looked around the library as if he had never noticed the bookshelves and comfy, worn chairs. She wondered what he wanted to talk about. "I didn't tell you about my accident," he said.

She raised her brows as her hand touched her cheek scar.

"I think you should know." He stopped as if collecting his thoughts. "It was a long time ago." He sighed, set down his coffee, and leaned back in his chair. "It was a foggy night. You know that stretch by the high school?"

She nodded, picturing the school on one side and a guardrail preventing motorists from driving off the steep embankment on the other. The same place where their accident took place—was that a coincidence?

"It was like pea soup, and I couldn't see my headlights. I think I had smoked pot with some friends before heading out. The visibility didn't seem to bother me. I'd never drive in thick fog now, but then, well, I did. The accident involved three cars. Someone from school named Leo didn't stay in his lane and ran headfirst into the guy Rob Larkin, and I slammed into the back of Rob's car. Leo and Rob were killed. I survived."

"And that's where you got the forehead scar?" Her hand twitched to reach over and run her fingers over his forehead, but she thought better and touched her cheek scar instead.

His eyes followed her fingers to her cheek. He hadn't missed her gesture and tilted his head infinitesimally to one side. "Yup."

"How did you feel afterward?"

"Confused." He took another sip of his coffee. "I understand what you feel, somewhat. I was a messed-up kid in high school, too. Although I didn't cause the accident, I was in the wrong place and at the wrong time. Probably like you."

"True. I was confused, too. Still am."

He quirked a brow at her, but she didn't elaborate.

"It took a long time to figure myself out after the accident. I changed. I went into the hospital as a stoner and came out—" He paused as if deciding what to say. "—different. The accident changed me into a sober man with goals to help others and get his life on track."

Very similar to what she felt.

He cleared his throat. "Did the doctors tell you you

had a concussion and head trauma?"

She nodded. Wondering where this was leading, if anywhere. "Could it be anything else?"

Was he trying to tell her he had a walk-in soul?

Henry opened his mouth as if to reply but then closed it and dipped his chin once, meaning what? Yes?

At that moment, Maxi and Charlotte ran over. "We're hungry, Daddy. We want pizza!"

"Yeah!" Charlotte said.

"Pizza?" He gave her a mock-stern look. "I was thinking about meatloaf."

The girls both made faces. Maxi stuck out her tongue.

"It's better for you than pizza," he said.

"Gross! Daddy! We don't want that!"

"Pizza it is." He put his hands on his knees and stood.

"Can Sabrina come too?" Maxi asked, grabbing Sabrina's hand and pulling her upright.

"Sure."

"Sabrina's going to be my new babysitter," Maxi told Charlotte.

"You already told me that," Charlotte said.

Sabrina watched their exchange.

Henry looked over Maxi's head to where Sabrina sat. "How about it, babysitter? You feel like pizza?"

Sabrina smiled. The atmosphere was light and fun. "Sure."

If what Olivia had told her was true, would Henry have invited her to pizza? She didn't think so.

They ordered a large cheese pizza at the pizza restaurant and sat at a round table. When their pizza arrived, they talked about what the girls were doing in school, the upcoming concert, and what they wanted to do on summer vacation. Henry gave the girls money to play video games in the play area when they finished eating, and they scampered off.

"Let's talk about you moving in."

"Are you sure about that?"

He frowned at her. "What's wrong?"

"Nothing, it's just that…" Sabrina scratched at the table in front of her.

"What?" His face was concerned but held a hint of annoyance.

"Are you just being nice because…well, you know…" Her words trailed off, and she continued to stare at the table connected to their booth.

"I'm not just being nice. I need you. I mean, we need you."

"Only if you're sure."

"I'm sure. Are you?" Henry asked, his eyes narrowed.

This conversation isn't going well.

"It's just that…" Sabrina considered her words. "Olivia said—"

"Don't," Henry interrupted, his tone sharp. "I mean, don't"—he gave her a small smile, speaking gently—"listen to what she says. She doesn't know our arrangement."

"Okay." Sabrina gave him a faint smile and looked up.

Henry reached over to squeeze her fingers. "I've got to clear out some junk piled in the guest bedroom. Do you have a lot of stuff?"

"No, not much." Sabrina admitted. "A garbage bag full."

"Any furniture?"

"None."

"We better go shopping for a bed and mattress. The one in there is old and a bit lumpy."

"I'm sure anything you pick out will be fine," she said.

"Nope." Henry wagged a finger. "I want your opinion."

She swallowed thickly. Little by little, her life was entangling with his—this time, in a good way. Would it stay that way? And what of Olivia? What would she think of this new living arrangement? Sabrina didn't think Olivia would leave the good doctor alone.

Chapter 24

The evening of Maxi and Charlotte's concert was breezy but clear. It was held at the Clearwater Elementary School auditorium, two blocks from the Heritage Apartments. Sabrina wore the turquoise blouse Henry liked. It was her nicest garment. She walked, breathing deeply—the fresh air always made her feel buoyant and happy. She was almost as excited as Maxi.

Although she wanted to hear Maxi's solo, she was more interested in seeing Henry. Lately, he filled her dreams at night with sensual images and long, intimate kisses. Just thinking about him now made her stomach tighten with anticipation. Would Olivia be there, too? Henry never mentioned her name, but she knew Brooklyn was also in Maxi's class.

Sabrina waited by the two sets of double doors for them to arrive. Already, parents, grandparents, siblings, and excited students arrived. Sabrina rubbed her arms. The concert was all Maxi talked about. She thought they'd be here by now. Finally, Henry and Maxi arrived. Maxi was wearing the dress Sabrina had given her.

"You look beautiful!" Sabrina said.

Maxi grinned. "I love my dress." She touched her hair and the sparkly band that kept the hair from her eyes. She twirled for Sabrina.

Henry squeezed Sabrina's hand. "Thank you for

coming—and giving her that dress. She always wants to wear it around the house and show me how cute she is."

"Are you kidding?" she said, feeling happy seeing Maxi's excitement over the thrift shop dress. It fit her perfectly. "All I've heard about for the last month is 'the concert.' "

He chuckled and rolled his eyes. "Ditto."

He probably had it ten times worse than she had.

Olivia and her daughter, Brooklyn, arrived next.

"Hi, Brooklyn," Maxi said, primly and without much enthusiasm.

Olivia studied Maxi. "We need to take you shopping, Honey. Did your daddy buy that for you?"

Maxi's eyes narrowed. "No! Sabrina gave me this. I love it! It's my favorite!"

Olivia raised her brows and shrugged. She turned to Henry and leaned in. Henry gave Olivia a peck on the cheek.

"Can't you do better than that?" Olivia asked with a frown.

Henry appeared not to have heard Olivia, and Maxi made motions of sticking a finger down her throat.

When Olivia saw Sabrina, she narrowed her eyes slightly but seemingly wore a bright mask. "Hello, Samantha. I didn't think you'd be here tonight."

"Her name is Sabrina," Henry replied tersely.

"Oh, dear, my mistake." Olivia's expression could only be described as simpering—a word Sabrina had learned from reading.

The girl had a silly, simpering smile on her face.

As an example, the dictionary would have a picture of Olivia to illustrate the meaning. "And why are you here exactly?" Olivia looked Sabrina up and down.

"Maxi invited me." Sabrina put a hand on Maxi's shoulder, which wasn't lost on Olivia, who narrowed her eyes even more.

"Where's your boyfriend?" Olivia asked. She was no longer simpering but catty, Sabrina thought.

"Who?" Sabrina asked.

"The guy at the Alcoholics Anonymous meeting." Olivia's voice rose when she said "Alcoholics Anonymous."

She remembered introducing Billy to Olivia at the library. "He's just a friend, and I don't attend AA."

Olivia spun around and said off-handedly to Brooklyn. "She could have fooled me!"

Brooklyn stared blankly at her mother.

Sabrina felt her face redden as several people stared at her. Olivia rubbed her hands together and looked at both girls. "Brookie," she said, "sweetheart, why don't you and Maxi go get ready?"

Brooklyn grabbed Maxi's hand, but Maxi shook it free. They ran down the hallway toward a growing number of students waiting to line up for the concert. Sabrina saw Maxi take Charlotte's hand instead. The noise rose as more students arrived—shrill screams, pounding feet, and teachers yelling above the din to line up.

"We better get a seat," Henry said, clearing his throat.

He seemed on edge, Sabrina noted by the slight crease between his brows. Was he worried about what Olivia might say or do? He hadn't acted tense until Olivia and Brooklyn arrived.

Olivia grabbed his arm possessively and gave Sabrina a look of triumph and superiority. Henry was

Olivia's, and she didn't want Sabrina to forget that. Henry untangled Olivia's arm from his, slowed, and motioned for Sabrina.

Olivia flounced off, but not before she gave Sabrina "the" stare. They found chairs in the middle of the fifth row. Henry sat between them, and Sabrina was glad.

"Where's your mother?" Olivia mock whispered to Henry as she shrugged out of her coat.

"Asthma attack. I told her not to come. I'll record it so she can see."

Henry pulled out his cell phone and trained it on the stage as the students began to file onto their places on the risers center stage.

Sabrina leaned forward as Maxi sang her solo from Annie—"The Sun Will Come Out Tomorrow." Her high, sweet voice projected over the audience. Sabrina would have been scared silly to sing in front of all these people, but Maxi seemed to relish it and bowed when she finished, and the crowd clapped and cheered. She couldn't wait to tell Maxi what a good job she'd done.

"She's a natural," Sabrina whispered to Henry. "I'm so proud of her!"

He reached over and squeezed her hand, and they lingered, their fingers intertwined for longer than necessary.

When Henry bent forward, Sabrina saw Olivia glare at her, then Olivia put her hand over Henry's and smiled so wide, her lipstick cracked. "Yes, bravo! Maxi did beautifully."

It was almost as if Olivia was one-upping Sabrina.

Henry suggested they go for ice cream when the concert finished, and Olivia seemed to have recovered her possessiveness toward Henry. "Shall we all go together? Or drive separately?"

"Separately," Henry said. But, knowing Sabrina didn't drive, he took her with them.

After they ordered, Olivia looked at Sabrina and asked, "And why are you here? This is *family time*. Who are you exactly?"

Henry let out a long, noisy sigh as if he was tired of Olivia's games. "She's Maxi's after-school sitter," Henry answered for her, dipping a napkin in water to clean Maxi's purple lips. "And Maxi"—Henry swiped Maxi's chin—"invited her."

Maxi was wiggling under Henry's grasp and eager to run around.

Olivia's brows arched. "You know I would be happy to take care of Maxi on my days off," Olivia said to Henry, ignoring Sabrina.

Maxi scooted closer to Sabrina. "No! I want Sabrina."

Sabrina stayed silent, allowing Maxi to lean on her.

Olivia arched a brow at Henry as if to say, "Aren't you going to say something?"

"I appreciate your offer. But you have Brooklyn to care for."

"Brookie and Maxi are friends."

Maxi rolled her eyes. "Not really."

"Brookie?" Olivia said, fake concern creasing her brow. "Say you're her friend."

Brooklyn looked to the ceiling with a grimace. "She's my friend." Brooklyn shoveled a big spoonful of ice cream into her mouth. "There!" she spoke with her mouth full. "Are you happy?"

"See!" Olivia said. "They're friends."

Henry was unconvinced and said, "She wants Sabrina so…"

"Children don't always know what's best for them. We as parents need to guide them," Olivia countered.

"We'll keep things the way they are," Henry said, to which Olivia shrugged and pursed her mouth.

They were interrupted by Charlotte and her parents' arrival.

Maxi jumped up and ran to hug Charlotte.

"I like your dress," Charlotte's mother said.

Maxi turned around to beam at Sabrina.

They pulled more chairs to their table so they could all be together. Sabrina ate her ice cream and listened to Olivia talk to the girls about using their napkins and minding their manners. Maxi and Charlotte had good manners. Brooklyn needed a refresher course—smacking her lips and dribbling ice cream on the table.

They finished their ice cream and stood to leave.

"Would you like to come over for a nightcap?" Olivia asked Henry.

"No, I'm tired." Henry faked a yawn, stretching both arms out. "Plus, Maxi needs to go to bed."

"You could spend the night? Brookie has a bunk bed."

"No, I don't think so," he said again, running his hands through his hair.

"Suit yourself," Olivia said. "Call me tomorrow?" Her voice was pleading.

Henry only dipped his chin and didn't respond.

Maxi yawned.

"Come on, sleepyhead!" Henry squeezed Maxi's shoulder. "Let's go home. Can I give you a lift?" He turned and looked questioningly at Sabrina.

"Yes. Please." Sabrina hitched up her pack and slid her chair under the table. "Thank you."

Henry guided them to his car. The 4EAEA license plate still intrigued her. She knew the meaning of the letters, but how did it come to be?

Henry saw her studying it. "It was Alison's license plate."

"I know. Forever and ever, always."

"How did you guess?"

"I don't know. What's special about it?"

A melody popped into her head. A song. The words of a song. "It was a song, wasn't it?" Sabrina tapped her chin. "Country," she said.

"Yes." Henry confirmed. "How'd you know? You don't strike me as a country music fan."

How did I know that? Another guess?

Sabrina yanked open the car door. "I just know," she said as she helped Maxi into the car booster and seatbelt. Maxi's head drooped, and Sabrina was sure she'd fall asleep soon. "You were wonderful tonight," she whispered, to which Maxi nodded.

When they arrived at Sabrina's place, Henry leaned toward her—she swore he was going to kiss her and she licked her lips in anticipation—when he popped open the door.

"It sticks, sometimes," he said.

He lingered there as she unbuckled her belt. As she predicted, Maxi was sound asleep and her little girl snores filled the silence. Sabrina awkwardly hugged him before exiting. She caught a whiff of his cologne and had the overwhelming urge to run her hands in his hair.

Get out of the car! Get out before you do

something embarrassing!

"Thanks for the ride." She tapped the door as she stood up. Sabrina leaned inside, before shutting it. "I hope you don't have far to go."

"No," Henry replied. "Elm and Church. Fairly close."

She knew that area with the neat front yards, wide porches, and cozy Craftsman style homes—Craftsman was a favorite housing design in that area. In fact, she and Billy had walked around there the day the library was closed due to cleaning.

"I like that part of town."

"Good, it will be where you live soon." He gave her a wink before driving off.

She watched him drive away, her gaze zeroed on the 4EAEA. She hoped she and Henry could be together that way, but was it possible? After all, she was the person that killed his wife. Could they even consider forever and ever, always? The odds were not in their favor.

Chapter 25

On Saturday, Henry picked Sabrina up to shop for furniture since she had nothing except a lumpy mattress and dresser, which was missing several drawers, at the apartment. She needed the works—bed, dresser, and nightstand. They drove to Grand Rapids—just the two of them.

Sabrina frowned when she saw the backseat was empty.

"Maxi decided it would be more fun to go to Grandma's and make cookies," Henry explained when Sabrina peered into the backseat looking for her.

Would the seven-year-old Sabrina have wanted to shop for furniture? Probably not. Sabrina imagined when Henry gave Maxi a choice; she wanted to make cookies and not do something boring like picking out bedroom furniture. But Sabrina missed Maxi's bright chatter about anything and everything.

It was nice to have Henry by herself, though. They were insulated in his car as they drove toward their destination—Mattress Universe and More.

"What do people think when you tell them you've hired me as a babysitter for Maxi?" Sabrina asked, moving her hands like she was applying lotion.

She might as well determine how she would be received. She knew Olivia didn't like her, but what of Henry's mother?

Henry kept his eyes on the road but tapped a finger on the wheel as if thinking about his answer.

"Most people don't know our connection."

"What about your mother?"

Henry cleared his throat. "She doesn't know you like Maxi and I do." He paused as if trying to find the right words. "She'll probably take some convincing. But she's working full-time, and we don't see as much of her as we'd like to. Unless she comes over unannounced, you probably won't see her."

Henry's mother needled at her. Beverly. Was her name Beverly?

"Her name's Beverly?" Sabrina asked although she was pretty sure about the name.

"Yes."

A memory of a woman named Beverly who didn't like her entered her mind—a woman with hair color similar to Henry's, but her mouth was set in a grim line, whereas Henry's lips were full and sensual. Henry must have gotten his lips from his father.

"Does she work at the bank?"

Henry had a look of surprise and doubt.

"I remember her not liking me," Sabrina said, twisting her hands together again.

"When did you meet her?"

Her mind whirled with the details of meeting Henry's mother. She shook her head. "I'm sure I have, but I can't remember when or how…" Sabrina chewed her lip.

Henry looked dubious before putting on his blinker, and they entered the parking lot of Mattress Universe and More.

They were distracted by the salesman who met

them at the door. "What can I help you find?"

"We need bedroom furniture," Henry said, guiding Sabrina forward with his hand near her lower back.

Sabrina looked around. The whole store was nothing but bedroom furniture and mattresses. It was overwhelming to see so much stuff crammed into such little space.

"What kind of firmness in a mattress do you folks like?"

Sabrina shrugged. She had been sleeping on uncomfortable mattresses forever. "Maybe medium?"

"Okay, then!" The salesman smiled brightly, rubbing his hands. "Let me show you what we have."

The salesman, named Brady, took them to mattresses of every size and firmness. He pointed to one. "Try this."

Sabrina sat on the edge before lying down. The mattress felt good on her back. She moved her shoulders so every part of her could feel it. It wasn't too firm or soft. It was just right, as Goldilocks would say.

"Why don't you try it, too?" Brady urged Henry to lie down.

The weight of his body made Sabrina roll toward him. Henry turned on his side, and they were nose to nose. He brushed her hair from his face. They were that close. His breathing quickened and Sabrina's hair fell back onto his face. Henry quickly rolled off and smacked it. "I like it."

"Well?" Brady asked her.

Henry turned to Sabrina with one brow raised, and she nodded, sitting up.

"We'll take this one!" Henry said to Brady.

"Don't you and your wife want to see any others?"

"She likes this one," Henry said again and patted it with his hand. Sabrina noticed Henry didn't correct Brady about their marital status.

Brady looked at the tag as he marked something down on his clipboard. "Lucky you." Brady whistled and motioned to the price tag. "It's on sale."

"Lucky us," Henry agreed. "Now furniture!" Henry shot an arm up like he was some superhero about to take flight.

Sabrina giggled as she eased off the mattress. Henry offered an arm saying, "Madam."

Brady smiled as he waved an arm over most of the center part of the store. "We've got every style and color you can imagine."

Sabrina walked toward the first display—white furniture. She didn't think so. *White is just so hard to keep clean—especially with a kid.*

The next was a medium color, plain with no frills. But Henry shook his head.

They walked around, touching furniture, using unspoken language, raising their brows, and moving their heads to judge what the other thought. Finally, they agreed on an oak set, plain in design, but sturdy—with a lovely grain pattern.

Henry opened and closed the drawers and squinted at the construction. "This looks well made."

"Amish," Brady said. "Their stuff is made to last."

"I like it," Sabrina said, her fingertips resting on the wood—it would last a long time. She hoped she'd last a long time, too. She wanted to be part of Henry's life for as long as this dresser.

Brady announced it was on sale, too. It seemed everything was on sale.

"How soon can we get this delivered?" Henry asked.

"How about two weeks from today?"

"Nothing sooner?" Henry asked. "We're kind of in a hurry."

"Three days." Brady nodded. "But it'll cost an extra fifty bucks."

"Sold!" Henry said and handed Brady his credit card.

While Henry finished the deal, Sabrina looked back at the beautiful set. She had never had new furniture before. Her parents mainly shopped at thrift stores or found abandoned furniture on the side of the road.

The whole process took about three hours.

"I could use a beer and some lunch," Henry announced.

Sabrina felt her stomach constrict at the mention of lunch and then a resounding gurgle. She laughed.

"Are you hungry?" he asked, grinning.

"That obvious?" Her stomach did another grumble, and Henry laughed.

"That makes two of us!"

They left the store and walked to Lotsa Burgers for lunch across the parking area. Inside, they each ordered burgers—Henry got a beer, and Sabrina had iced tea.

"I like the bedroom set. Thank you," Sabrina said again as she unwrapped the straw and swirled some sugar into her tea.

"I'm glad you'll be moving in to help with Maxi. She's excited, you know." Henry took a long swallow of his beer. "She said it was almost like having a mother."

"Poor girl." Sabrina frowned. "I'll be the best surrogate mother to her."

"I know you will." He reached across the table and squeezed her fingers. Their hands remained that way until the waitress brought their burgers.

Sabrina wondered what the handholding meant if anything. Did he feel the same sizzle when they touched as she had?

Henry was a nice guy, and yes, she was falling in love with him, but did he feel the same way? As far as she could tell, he was still dating Olivia. But Henry said Maxi would have the last word on a partner. And since Maxi didn't like Olivia or her daughter, Brooklyn…

Chapter 26

Sabrina packed her meager clothing in a black garbage bag three days later and waited for Henry and Maxi to pick her up.

Then she got a text from her mother. —*Do you have any extra cash to send us? We're in a bind*—

Sabrina ignored the plea for money and looked out the apartment window and saw Henry's sedan. She hurried downstairs with her bag. Henry stowed it in the trunk. "Is this it?" he asked.

"That's it."

He only raised his brows, but didn't comment further.

The streets became more familiar as they drove, and memories flooded her mind. A young girl on a bicycle, her father helping her down the sidewalk. She seemed to remember her and her mother decorating the front porch for Christmas and making Christmas cookies...A tiny part of her knew she didn't grow up here, but something pushed it aside—a knowing she had.

The closer they got to their destination, the more she remembered. When they pulled into the drive, Sabrina knew this was the house she and Billy had stopped at several months before. Even then, memories popped into her mind. Now, they were more apparent and not some hazy outlines.

"We're home!" Maxi announced.

Sabrina must have had a peculiar expression because Henry turned to her and said, "Everything all right?"

"What?" The murkiness in her brain receded, but it crouched at the perimeter ready to pounce again.

"You look like you've seen a ghost or something."

"Oh, no, I've always liked this house. I love it." Inside, her mind and emotions swirled.

Henry continued to stare at her. "This was Alison's childhood home. I wanted Maxi to live in a place that was near and dear to her mother."

Sabrina swallowed several times, trying to dislodge the lump in her throat. Maxi got out, ran around to Sabrina's door, and tugged it open. "Come on! I'll show you around!"

Pink tulips poked out of the ground at the side where they parked. "Pink tulips," Sabrina murmured—she loved pink tulips.

"They were my mom's favorite," Maxi said in a sing-song voice as they exited the car, and she took Sabrina's hand.

"Pink tulips are my favorites, too." Sabrina longed to smell them. With a backward glance, she let Maxi pull her up the steps while Henry unlocked the door. It was as if time had stopped when she stepped into the living room—the blue chair and couch—all as she remembered. Her breath seemed stuck in her throat. She half expected to see her mother come out of the kitchen.

It didn't smell the same—not the cinnamon, coffee, and fabric softener she remembered. Instead, now there were notes of lemon, green grass, and Maxi's shampoo—a pleasant mix for the senses—just different.

She stopped as voices and images came at her from all angles, and voices spoke to her—yelling. Sabrina felt claustrophobic and unbalanced as if the house was tilting—a tornado swirling through the rooms.

"Come on!" Maxi continued to pull her toward the hallway.

"No, I can't."

Maxi looked confused. "What's wrong?"

"It's just that…" How do you explain to a seven-year-old that she was remembering the past as Alison? How did she even explain it to herself? Or Henry?

Maxi continued to tug on her.

"Sabrina?" Henry asked.

"I…I feel so strange."

He nodded and came over and studied her face.

"What's the matter?" he asked.

The tears started. "I remember it all."

"All what?" His brows furrowed with concern.

"Living here as Alison." There, she said it, the elephant in the room. "That's what I've been trying to figure out. I think I'm her."

Henry watched her but didn't speak. Maxi also looked concerned, and she dropped Sabrina's hand.

"I'm sorry." Sabrina tried to swallow her sobs. "I don't know if I can do this."

She hugged herself. Her stomach felt as if it might explode.

"Don't you want to see my room?" Maxi said in a tiny voice.

"Of course I do, Pet." She put her palm on the wall to steady herself. "I'm just a little dizzy, that's all."

Henry turned her around and pushed her gently into the nearest chair. "Let's give Sabrina a moment to get used to our house. We'll show her later."

Now Maxi looked like she would cry, too, but Henry led her away, his hand on her shoulder. Sabrina saw Maxi's tear-streaked face as she turned to look at her.

The white noise of the house grabbed her and smothered her—memories came at her like ghosts, swooping eerily. She squeezed her eyes shut, but still she saw them—her mother toppled over in the chair and her death while the paramedics worked frantically to save her—despair and sadness washed over Sabrina. She was surrounded in suffocating blackness, and she couldn't quite catch her breath. She had grown up in this house. Gradually, she stopped sniffling, and the hiccups subsided. She eased out of the chair. She heard an undercurrent of voices coming from down the hall—Henry speaking to Maxi. The voices in her head had roared, but they eventually quieted. She went down the hall to what she assumed was Maxi's bedroom. It had once been Alison's as well.

She stopped outside the closed door and listened, breathing deeply to steady her hammering heart.

"Sabrina is having a hard time right now," she heard Henry tell Maxi.

"Why? Daddy? Why?"

"A lot has happened to her, and we need to help her settle here."

"I want to help her!" Maxi said.

"I know you do."

Sabrina knocked softly on the door. "Can I come in?"

Henry opened the door, and Sabrina rushed to sit next to Maxi and put her arm around her. "I'm sorry I upset you, Pet. It's just that I've never lived in a nice house like this before. I guess I got dizzy and confused."

Maxi nodded as Sabrina talked. Sabrina glanced toward Henry to gauge if she was saying the right things to Maxi. She mouthed "my mother."

He dipped his chin as if he understood her dilemma.

"This is your room, right, Pet?" Maxi's tears stopped. "It's a wonderful room." She looked up and down and all around before declaring, "I love it!"

Maxi's bedroom had been Alison's. It had been blue once, and now, it was pink. But it still had the same lacy curtains and louvered doors on the closet where Alison had once played hide and seek or with her dolls and teddy bears.

Maxi grinned. "Do you want to see your room?"

Sabrina stood and held out her hand. "Show me."

Maxi tugged on her hand, and they went to the room next door.

The doorbell sounded.

"I think the furniture is here," Henry said.

"Will you help me get settled?" Sabrina asked Maxi, surveying the mostly empty room. The closet door was open with some hangers on the pole. Sheets, blankets, and pillows occupied the closet shelf.

She heard the movers thumping down the hallway with the furniture and Henry's voice directing them where to put it. When the movers came in lugging the mattress, Sabrina and Maxi stepped into the hall.

"Do you want to see the rest of the house?" Maxi asked.

"Maybe later, after we've put my clothes away and

made the bed."

They watched the procession of mattress, headboard, and chests disappear into her new room.

She wasn't sure she wanted to see her parents' bedroom. No, she squeezed her eyes shut; she wasn't up to that.

"Okay, but Daddy's room is at the end of the hall, and the kitchen is over there." Maxi pointed.

"You can show me later."

Sabrina steeled herself to see her parents' bedroom. She pushed the memories away of climbing into bed with them when she had a nightmare and...No, she would look later. Her mind quieted finally and she could reacquaint herself with the house little by little.

Chapter 27

"Do you like your new room, Sabrina?" Maxi asked.

"I do, Pet. It's the nicest room I've ever had." She smoothed down the comforter on the bed. Henry thought to buy bedding even. The picture once over the fireplace mantel now resided in the guest bedroom—Sabrina's for the time being.

Maxi considered her words with a frown. "Didn't you ever have a pink bedroom like mine?"

"No." Sabrina's thoughts ping-ponged to the apartment she had abandoned with its spare furnishings, like all their previous lodgings, and her blue childhood bedroom when she had been Alison.

"Why not?"

"My parents were poor and didn't have nice things."

Maxi moved her mouth. "Did they have jobs?"

"Sometimes."

"My daddy has a job, and my mother was a teacher."

"Yes, she was," Sabrina said. She heard a creak of a footstep in the hall and saw Henry's shadow. He was listening to their conversation.

"Did you know her?" Maxi asked.

"No, but your daddy told me about her. She sounded like a very special person." Sabrina gave

Maxi's shoulders a light squeeze.

Maxi's lips puckered. "I wish I had a mother."

"I do, too. Can I help in that regard? Be a pretend mother to you?"

Maxi nodded vigorously, and Sabrina heard another creak as Henry shifted in the hallway.

"Would you like to get on the bed, and we'll read a story?" Sabrina asked.

"Oh, yes, can we read *Charlotte's Web*! I'll get it!" Maxi ran into the hallway. "Daddy!"

Sabrina heard an "oomph" from Henry. Had Maxi run into him?

Sabrina listened as Maxi's bedroom door opened, and papers were rustling.

"You were in the hallway?" she asked Henry who now stood in the doorway.

He rubbed his thigh. "Yes, and Maxi about knocked me over."

"You should have come in."

"No, you had a nice way of handling things with Maxi," Henry said, looking down at her.

She felt her eyes fill with tears. "I feel so bad for what happened, and I know I'll never be able to make it up to her or you." She studied her hands clasped in her lap.

She felt his hand on her shoulder.

"When she's older, maybe we can tell her about the circumstances surrounding Alison's death and her birth."

"You mean…the walk-in soul part?" The part she had only just realized.

"Yes. And maybe I can tell her about my walk-in soul."

"You?" She looked up at him.

"I switched with Robert."

"Robert?" Sabrina asked. Robert who?

"Yes, Robert, Rob, as in Alison's Rob." He straightened.

"Daddy? Where's my backpack?" Maxi called.

He stepped back. "We'll talk more." And called, "By the front door on the hook!" He turned back to her.

Sabrina heard Maxi run down the hallway. She and Henry studied each other. What was she to think of his revelation? He was Rob, and she was Alison. How could that be? She didn't know what to think. Her mind refused to go there, yet it remained frozen in place.

When Maxi rushed in, Henry patted Sabrina's shoulder.

The refrain of "we'll talk more" seemed to be the gist of most of their conversations.

"I got it!" Maxi exclaimed, waving the book and launching herself on the bed.

"I'll let you two read," Henry said, backing away. His face was unreadable to her—blank even, the face a doctor might need to talk to a patient. He closed the door softly behind him.

They settled in to read. Maxi read one page and Sabrina the next. She sighed deeply. It was wonderful to have Maxi by her side—her daughter—her heart. And Henry? He was part of her heart, too. Something told her this was what forever love was like—peaceful and giving.

Chapter 28

Gradually, Sabrina reacquainted herself with most of the house. She wasn't ready to visit the bedroom at the end of the hall—the one her parents shared, and now Henry occupied. Would it be the same? She glimpsed the bed and comforter through the open doorway—that was different, but she averted her eyes, not ready for those memories. Her parents' bed covering was blue and white. Henry favored more neutral tones, but she saw a hint of blue.

Parts of the house were different, though. Henry had put a new cushion on the window seat near the dining room and had installed a large screen television over the fireplace where there was once a picture of Lake Michigan. But essentially, the house felt as if she had never left.

She wanted to stop every few steps to remember and take in the objects and furniture in each room. But if she stepped closer to the bedroom at the end of the hallway, the noise began to swirl around her sucking her toward the doorway. She fought the urge to go farther, but it was as if invisible hands pushed her along.

"No!"

The noise continued to swirl around her sucking her farther into the room.

In the master's doorway, Sabrina stopped, focused

on the blue chair, and said, "Mother!" Images of her mother toppled over, her book splayed with its pages, moving in the air. She rushed toward the chair to protect her mother from falling but couldn't.

Her mother was on the floor, and her skin was cold. Sabrina yanked the blanket from the bed to cover her. "Mother!" The room spun around.

"Who are you talking to?" Maxi asked.

Sabrina's vision swam until it went black.

From far away, she heard, "Daddy! Something's wrong with Sabrina! She's falling!"

Sabrina felt herself tipping over. Is this what her mother felt when she toppled off this chair after having a heart attack? The carpeted floor jarred her elbow as she hit the floor. She hugged herself and moaned. *Oh, Mother, how I miss you!*

She felt Henry's arms cradling her and leaned heavily into him, comforted by his familiar smells of hair gel and the wool of his sweater. She felt soothed and loved in her pain.

"Let's get you in the chair." He kept his arms around her, slowly raising her, and eased her into the chair.

"This chair…My mother."

"Get me a wet washcloth," Henry said to Maxi, still keeping his arms around Sabrina. "I want to have you checked out," he said. "Maxi, can you get my stethoscope from the closet too?" He used the light from his phone to look into her eyes. He held up a finger. "Can you track my finger?"

She did as he commanded, but the light made her blink, and tears pooled at the corners.

"I don't think you have a concussion," he said,

putting his phone in his pocket. His hands moved in her hair, feeling for lumps. "Does that hurt?"

"No, not really." She winced when he found a tender spot. "Right there."

His fingers stilled and moved in a circle.

"It does feel like you have a contusion. How did this happen?"

"I was dizzy."

"Did it come on you suddenly?"

"Yes, I remembered…" Sabrina gripped the arms of the chair. "I remembered something horrible that happened in this room."

Henry's face was close to hers, and she could see the concern and confusion in his eyes.

"My mother died while in this chair."

"I thought your parents…" He stopped and studied her. "Your. Mother? Alison's mother?"

She nodded dumbly. "I know it sounds crazy, but I remember finding her."

He smoothed back her hair and put his arms around her. "It's not crazy." His lips kissed her forehead.

"But I remembered stuff that didn't happen to me," she said, touching her chest. "Me, Sabrina."

"I know. They happened to Alison." His voice was low and soft, and she leaned into his words and broad shoulders.

"How did…" She remembered Henry telling her he had Rob's soul.

"It took a while to figure it out," he admitted.

"Yes." His shirt collar was wet where she rested her face, tears soaking through the fabric.

She touched the wet splotches before sinking back into him. She never wanted to leave the comfort and security of his arms.

"Daddy!" Maxi reappeared, dangling a blue cloth in one hand and his stethoscope in the other.

He smiled. "Thank you." Tenderly, he wiped away her tears with the cloth soaked in cool water before smoothing back her hair. "All better?"

Sabrina nodded.

He helped her stand and led her to the bed. "Lie down while I check you over."

He checked her pulse and shined the light from his phone into her eyes again as if making sure before opening her shirt and checking her heart. The stethoscope was cold against her skin, and she shivered.

Henry reached down and pulled a blanket over her. "I want you to rest."

"Am I…"

"Your heart sounds good. Are you feeling better?"

"A bit."

The chaotic scene faded into black and white and then to a murky gray. Her mother's death left her, but thoughts and questions still lingered. She wished Henry would finish telling her about his exchange with Robert, but he didn't. His eyes told her they would finish their discussion when Maxi wasn't around. But he and Maxi stayed by her side, plying her with tea and tissues, and she gradually stopped hiccupping and sniffing.

Maxi smoothed the blanket around her and asked, "Are you going to be okay?" She put her hands on either side of Sabrina's face.

"I am." She struggled to sit up. "Thank you, Pet. I feel one hundred percent better."

Henry pushed her gently back into the pillows.

"Nurse Maxi, you're in charge of our patient!"

Maxi giggled. "You have to stay in bed. Daddy says so."

Sabrina nodded, relaxed into Henry's bed, and closed her eyes, trying to block out the images that continued to play hide and seek in her head.

"Can I read you a story?" Maxi asked.

"I'd like that."

Maxi brought several well-read and much-loved books and began reading. Sabrina remembered these books from her other childhood. Her biological parents never read to her.

Henry returned and felt her forehead. "How are you feeling?"

The truth was, she felt foolish. "Better." She pushed aside the blanket and tried to sit up.

"No." Henry tugged the blanket back on her. "You need to rest."

The doorbell sounded.

"I'll get it!" Maxi called, her feet padding down the hallway.

"Hi, Maxi," Sabrina heard Brooklyn say.

Had Henry been expecting Olivia?

He muttered, "Oh, shit."

No, I guess not. Sabrina covered her smile.

"Where's your father?" Olivia asked.

"He's taking care of Sabrina."

There was a long pause. "Where are you, Henry?" Olivia called out, her voice rising to an unnatural pitch.

"In here."

Sabrina heard the resignation in his voice as he got off the edge of the bed and started toward the hallway.

"What's she doing here?" Olivia met him at the

bedroom door, stopping inside the doorway. Her eyes bulged as she saw Sabrina in his bed.

"I told you, Sabrina's Maxi's babysitter." Henry sounded frustrated.

"I see what's going on here!"

"You clearly don't!" he said. "She was faint."

"I bet!"

Sabrina waved a hand to jump into the conversation but couldn't find an opening.

"I don't believe that B.S. for one minute!" Olivia shouted. "Are you sleeping with her?"

Henry pushed Olivia toward the hallway and closed the bedroom door. His response was muffled.

Sabrina sat back against the headboard and listened. She heard a scuffle in the hallway, a slap, and Olivia's angry voice got louder.

"I think you better leave, Olivia," Henry demanded.

"Oh, so I'm to blame now?" Olivia asked.

"No one's to blame. I told you. Sabrina moved into the guest room and cares for Maxi. She got dizzy, that's all."

"What's she doing in your bed?"

"You better go," Henry said.

"Why doesn't she go?"

"She lives here now."

"Well…isn't that rich! Good riddance to you, Dr. Comstock!"

Sabrina heard loud, angry footsteps echo in the hallway and a slam of the front door.

Henry entered the bedroom. "I'm sorry," he said.

"She's gone," Maxi whispered as she tiptoed in.

With resignation, Sabrina struggled off the bed.

The house and this room whispered to her, reminding her of the past. She pushed those thoughts aside, but while they still murmured, they were fainter now. She needed to live in the present and plan for the future. Sabrina pushed the memories back, but they would never be forgotten.

Henry had a red mark on his face.

"What happened to your face?" Sabrina asked.

"A good old-fashioned slap." He rubbed his face. "I guess she told me off!"

How awful.

"I'm so sorry," Sabrina said—remorse weighed down her words.

Is this arrangement even going to work?

Was this her punishment for the accident? To have the soul of a woman who loved and cherished this house and its occupants? Sabrina wanted to know the love of a man and a child too.

Henry kissed her forehead and hugged her tight and then laughed. "You're not crazy!" He kissed her forehead again, saying, "Don't you see? You're Alison! I'm Rob! We found each other again." He paused. "And again."

She liked the feeling of his lips on her head. *But what would it feel like to have a real kiss—lips to lips?* Sabrina blushed at the thought.

"But we need to talk," he said.

Uh oh.

She gulped and nodded.

Chapter 29

"I'm sorry I upset your girlfriend," Sabrina said the following morning. Sorry, but not sorry. Henry was reserved and friendly, but Olivia's rant had put a dark cloud over their household. She hadn't slept well either, tossing and turning, remembering Olivia's icy blue eyes with daggers of hate. If this had been a comic strip, Olivia would have lightning bolts coming from her eyes.

He moved his hand as if dismissing her comment. "It was on its last leg anyway."

She packed Maxi's lunch for school and made breakfast. Breakfast consisted of yogurt, cereal, and fruit for Maxi, toast and coffee for her and Henry. She'd have to study the cookbooks she found in the kitchen and make some new recipes.

He helped himself to more coffee, sat down, and ran his hand through his hair and looked like he had something more to say.

Was this "the talk"?

"It wasn't going to work with Olivia. Maxi didn't like her or Brooklyn. Whoever I date has to have Maxi's approval, and Olivia didn't have it." He smiled at her. "I wasn't sure how to tell her it was over. Thank you."

She gave him a dubious look. "Really? I thought you wouldn't want me here after last night. Is that what

165

you wanted to tell me last night when you said we needed to talk?"

"No, something else." He looked over at Maxi, who was slurping the milk from her cereal. "We also need to be a-l-o-n-e," he spelled, looking at Maxi. "Someplace with just the two of us."

"You sound serious."

He nodded but didn't elaborate, then left for work before she could question him further.

When Henry left, Sabrina and Maxi finished getting her backpack ready and finding coats and shoes. Part of her thoughts were on Maxi and the other on what they needed to discuss. He said it wasn't about Olivia, then what?

Sabrina put on her sneakers and jean jacket to walk Maxi to school. Maxi skipped and sang a nonsensical tune as they walked.

They walked to the area where students lined up before the bell sounded. Olivia and Brooklyn were already there. Brooklyn stuck her tongue out at Maxi, and Maxi returned the gesture.

"Maxi?" Sabrina whispered. "That's not very nice." But secretly, she was happy. Happy Maxi had stood up to Brooklyn.

"She did it first!"

True, Sabrina said silently. But Maxi had better manners than Brooklyn.

Olivia clapped. "Everyone!" She shouted and clapped. "Meet Maxi's babysitter, Sabrina. She's an alcoholic and ex-con!"

All eyes turned toward them, and Sabrina felt her cheeks flush. Several of the parents stepped back like she had COVID-19 or the plague and put their arms around their kids lest she kidnap them. Maxi squeezed her hand, and Sabrina studied the sidewalk cracks and the scuffed toes of her sneakers. Inside, her mind churned. Would she always have "ex-con" hanging over her head? Maybe it would be better to move away somewhere no one knew her?

"What did she mean?" Maxi asked, tears welling and threatening to spill over. "What's an alcoholic?"

"No worries. Don't cry." Sabrina slipped her arm around Maxi and wished she could take back Olivia's words. "She's being mean," Sabrina said quietly. The ex-con part was true, but she didn't want to explain that to Maxi here and now. "An alcoholic is someone who drinks too much."

"I bet you wanted to stick your tongue out at her," Maxi said, her eyes still flashing, watching Olivia and Brooklyn laugh at something hilarious.

Or give Olivia the finger. Sabrina chuckled. "I guess." She hugged Maxi. "Have a good day, Pet, and forget what Olivia said." The finger would prove Olivia right—that Sabrina was a low-life.

The bell sounded, the doors opened, and she breathed a long sigh.

Sabrina watched Olivia hurry away, get into her red sports car, and give Sabrina the finger before peeling away. *Now, who's the low-life?*

Sabrina walked back to the house slowly, thinking about all that had transpired in the last few months. She had gone from prison to her parents' apartment to Henry's house. The whole situation felt unreal, like a fairytale or a merry-go-round ride. Was Henry her Prince Charming? If he kissed her, would she turn into a princess? Or would she always have an "L" on her forehead for loser?

She returned to the house and wandered from room to room, running her fingers over familiar furniture and fixtures, all the while her mind replaying videos of memories. The voices and swirling mass of blackness had receded. What if she wasn't Alison? The books she read had confirmed she was. She had pretty much convinced herself, but what of Henry? Would he believe Sabrina was his dead wife, Alison? Their conversations about the topic had only touched the perimeter. How exactly could she prove herself?

She flopped into her favorite blue chair in the living room, closed her eyes, leaned back, and pinched her nose. A headache was gathering storm clouds at her temples.

When the ache behind her eyes subsided, she straightened and studied the books on the shelves that flanked the fireplace. She recognized some of the volumes—titles her parents liked. Her father's *For Whom the Bell Tolls* and her mother's *The Heart is a Lonely Hunter*.

But there were others, classics she had read in college when she was working on her English teaching credentials—*Little Women*, *Pride and Prejudice*, *Classroom Pedagogy*, and others. But did remembering books prove anything? It did to her because she hadn't grown up with a bookshelf of volumes to read and reread. Sabrina could never remember her parents having a book, newspaper, or magazine at their apartments.

Maybe they had the want ads, but that wasn't for reading about what was happening in the world or Michigan. Her parents' world was pretty narrow—

taking pleasure in drinking or doing drugs. Did they even know what was happening outside?

Her fingers continued gliding over the titles. There were medical books, Henry's—*Anatomy 105, Pharmacology for Physicians*...And then one caught her eye. It was small and had a turquoise cover—*Wandering Souls and Indigo Children.*

Her fingers trembled as she reached for the *Wandering Souls* book. She sat and opened it and perused the contents. Her eyes skimmed the text. Nothing was new; what she read only solidified her growing understanding of what had happened to Alison and her. Henry had read the book too when he learned about Robert.

She looked up at the clock. It was only eleven thirty, and she had three hours before she picked up Maxi from school.

She restlessly moved from room to room again, still avoiding the primary bedroom, the memories crowding all logical thought. Did she really need further validation?

Where did Henry keep records? She remembered a box of papers and files he moved from the guest bedroom to the hall closet. Maybe there was something in that box.

She pulled the box from the closet, sat on the floor, and went through the papers. Sabrina found the usual things people kept: marriage license, death certificate, and insurance policies. She ran her fingers over the official document for his marriage to Alison and an image of a pregnant Alison and Henry standing before a judge at the courthouse. Alison was pregnant with Maxi when they got married.

Sue C. Dugan

And then there were school records, his GED certificate, M-CAT scores, and a medical school diploma: Dr. Henry B. Comstock. How had Henry jumped over getting a bachelor's degree and attending medical school? His M-CAT score was 517—that was the reason.

She remembered sitting at the kitchen table, the same table they used now, quizzing him, her tongue tripping over medical terms and chemistry equations. How did someone with a poor record in high school go right to medical school, unless he had already gone to college before.

And what of Sabrina? She'd woken up from her coma with different beliefs, desires, and memories. The doctors diagnosed her with head trauma, but now she believed she had Alison's soul in her body. She had lived in this house—Alison's childhood home. She knew that there was a burned spot on the bedroom carpet where she had put her curling iron. Did Henry know it was there? Did Maxi?

She entered Maxi's bedroom, pushed aside a chair, and got down on her hands and knees to look for the spot. It was right where she remembered it.

There was that, but she wanted more. She wanted to be a teacher, and Alison was a teacher. And then there was Maxi. She couldn't explain the protectiveness she felt toward the girl. Sabrina didn't think that it was normal for a stranger to have those feelings for a child unless…unless they were the parent or some psycho (which she was pretty sure she wasn't).

She surveyed the papers and files she had pulled from Henry's box. Should she confess she had snooped through his things? Or see what he wanted to talk to her about? Would he like her to search for answers when he was at work? Sabrina knew she wouldn't like it. She gathered all the papers, put them in their folders, and returned the box to the closet.

She straightened and looked around. It was almost time to get Maxi from school. Her stomach grumbled, and she realized she had missed lunch. Henry would want dinner. She hadn't thought of what to make with her memories crowding aside all the mundane day-to-day routine. The voices stopped shouting in her head, and she could care for Maxi and Henry and not dwell in the past.

She went into the kitchen and looked in the freezer. There was a package of assorted chicken pieces. Maybe she'd take that out. But what would she do with them? Should she bother Henry at work? She remembered her other mother — Alison's mother—making chicken with a cracker crumb crust.

She texted Henry:

—Would you like me to fix dinner?—

—That would be nice.—

—I found chicken.—

—We like chicken.—

So chicken it would be. She could have Maxi help her. She searched further in the refrigerator and found a head of broccoli and some baking potatoes. They'd have chicken, baked potatoes, and broccoli for dinner.

Hardly gourmet, but it would satisfy them. Sabrina knew from helping in the prison kitchens that spices did wonders for food. She searched the cupboards and found the requisite salt and pepper, onion, garlic powder, and Italian seasonings. Yes, those would take plain, old chicken to the next level.

While she prepared dinner, her phone pinged again. Was it from Henry?

No, her father. —*Help! Send us $$ ASAP*—

Didn't they remember she was still paying restitution? She doubted they did.

Chapter 30

Sabrina walked to the school to retrieve Maxi, and while she walked, she kept an eye out for Olivia and Brooklyn. Thankfully, she didn't run into them. When she and Maxi walked home, Maxi talked about her day and what she and Charlotte did at recess.

"Do you want to help me make dinner?" Sabrina asked after Maxi had a snack and finished learning the words for the spelling test.

Maxi's eyes widened. "Yes! Charlotte helps her mother all the time."

Sabrina gave Maxi a tight smile. The poor kid just wanted a mother. But was having an ex-con mother with the soul of her biological mother the same? She'd try her best to be everything to Maxi.

Maxi grabbed the defrosted chicken and grinned back at Sabrina. "It's like having a mother, isn't it?"

Sabrina nodded and bit her lower lip to keep from crying. But instead of bursting into tears, she said, "I thought we'd fix your daddy chicken, potatoes, and broccoli. I know he likes those things."

Sabrina tipped her head to the side. How did she know his appetites? *Everyone likes those things, right?*

Together, they prepared the chicken and potatoes for baking and would boil the broccoli closer to when Henry got home. While they waited for him, Sabrina quizzed Maxi on the spelling words again.

"Can you use those words in a sentence?"

Maxi screwed her mouth as she thought. "Charlotte and Maxi took a pale blue pail to the beach." Maxi stopped and seemed pleased with herself. "Now you, Sabrina!"

Sabrina studied the words again. "Sabrina giggled at the musical on the stage."

At 5:45, Sabrina put the broccoli in the water to boil. She surveyed the kitchen and felt satisfied that this was the kind of environment an average family had. She remembered sitting at the exact table and eating with her parents; farther back in her mind, she remembered the fast food dinners her other parents ate. The two situations were vastly different. She wanted Maxi to have the childhood Alison had enjoyed.

At almost six, Henry came in and shrugged off his coat. Maxi ran to him. "Daddy!"

"Hi there, Punkin!" He swept her up in his arms. "How was school?"

"I played with Charlotte!"

"All day?" He joked and carried her to the kitchen. "Smells good!"

At that moment, car lights flashed in their driveway. Someone was coming. She certainly hoped it wasn't Olivia. But—*sigh*—it was. Her heels gave her away as she stomped up to the door.

The bell sounded, and Henry put Maxi down, shooting them both a quizzical look before opening the door for her. He started to say something, but Olivia held up her hand.

"I need to apologize for last night."

Henry nodded but didn't respond.

"I'm so sorry about the way I acted." Olivia forced

a smile at Maxi and Sabrina standing in the hallway.

Sabrina instinctively put her arm around Maxi—a protective move a mother would make when she perceived a threat.

Was she going to apologize for her behavior at the school, too? And for giving Sabrina the finger?

"Can we go someplace quiet and talk?" Olivia asked.

Apparently, Olivia wanted to apologize to Henry and not her.

Henry nodded, led Olivia to the living room, moved his head toward the kitchen, and raised his brows to Sabrina. She guessed his meaning—take Maxi to the kitchen so he could talk to Olivia privately.

"Come on, Pet, help me get dinner finished."

Sabrina used an oven mitt to check the chicken. It was browning nicely on the top and almost done. She used a fork to check the texture of the potatoes.

"What do you want me to do?" Maxi asked.

Sabrina was giving Maxi a fork when she heard Olivia's raised voice. "Oh, dear, that doesn't sound good," she said more to herself than to Maxi.

Maxi shrugged. "She and Daddy always fight."

"Oh?" Sabrina pretended not to care as she took the plates from the cupboard. "You can set the table."

"For us?" Maxi moved her foot in a windshield back and forth motion. "Is Olivia staying, too?"

The voices in the living room got louder, and Sabrina stiffened. She strained to make out some of Olivia's words: slut, felon, child protective services, and liar. She didn't think Olivia would stay for dinner.

Maxi frowned at the angry voices. "She's not very nice to Daddy."

"Oh?" Sabrina raised her eyebrow. "Why not? What kind of fights do they have?"

"Olivia wants to marry Daddy."

"I see."

"I don't like her."

"I know, Pet." Sabrina didn't like her either.

While they waited for Olivia to leave, Sabrina took the broccoli from the pan and placed it in a bowl while Maxi set plates and silverware on the table. She sprinkled some lemon pepper on the broccoli for a little zing and hoped Henry would like it.

Sabrina prayed the fight would end soon or everything would be cold.

"Where did you learn to cook?" Maxi asked, swinging her leg back and forth.

Sabrina stiffened again when she heard Henry's angry voice.

Maxi rolled her eyes. "Sucks to be Olivia."

Sabrina laughed softly. Yes, it sucked to be Olivia.

Soon after, they heard the door slam and Henry's heavy footsteps in the hall leading to the kitchen. He stood in the doorway, his hands on either side of the frame as if supporting himself and shook his head. "Well, that's that."

"Did you break up with her, Daddy?"

"I think so."

Maxi clapped her hands.

Sabrina frowned. "Will she be back?"

He ran his fingers through his hair. "I hope not, but maybe. She's a very persistent woman, but she's not the woman for me or Maxi." He stepped forward and mussed Maxi's hair. "Right, Punkin?"

"Right." Maxi smoothed down her hair.

"Something smells delicious in here." He sniffed the air by Maxi. "Is it you?" He pretended to try to bite Maxi's arm, making her giggle.

"Daddy!" she cried. "It's chicken!"

"Oh, I thought we were having Maxi!"

Sabrina turned from the stove and smiled at Henry and Maxi. For the moment, things were good and right.

Chapter 31

The whispers of the house mainly held good memories for Sabrina now. As she went about her daily chores when Maxi was in school, and Henry was at work, she listened to the memories of the past.

This house had seen all sorts of monumental events. As she gathered Maxi's clothing to do laundry, she looked out the window and remembered a boy coming into her bedroom window at night. They were only in high school but had already decided they would marry someday. She wore his class ring on a chain around her neck. Oh, and she remembered, they had done some heavy necking in high school, mainly in the backseat of his car, but wanted to take it to the next level—they were both virgins.

She remembered waiting in her bedroom for the knock on her window. Alison had stayed still, barely breathing, wanting his hands on all of her intimate parts. She felt her heart quicken as she remembered one backseat encounter where they had almost had sex. Tonight was their night.

Sabrina felt her cheeks warm as she descended into the basement to go to the washing machine. The dim space held a laundry room and boxes and bins of memories.

Sabrina loaded the washing machine and paused as she surveyed the basement—bare cinderblocks with tiny rectangular windows that let in weak sunlight. It wasn't an inviting place—dark and filled with shadows from below the house. But it held within its keep boxes of pictures, mementos, and other things stored on the top shelf and marked "china."

The timer on the stove buzzed. Sabrina looked at the clock. She needed to see Becki and Chuck for her parole meeting and support group. She hurried upstairs, grabbed her backpack, and walked briskly to Becki's office.

"How's the new job going?" Becki asked when Sabrina came in and sat down. Sabrina had graduated to every other week for these sessions.

"It's going." It was wonderful and terrible at the same time—wonderful to be with Maxi and Henry daily, but terrible in people's judgment about the situation. Couldn't people mind their own business?

"Are you getting pushback?"

Big time!

"Yes. You know, I'm nannying full-time now."

Becki shuffled her notes. "For the man whose wife was killed in the accident?"

"The one and only."

"I can imagine how that's perceived in this place." Becki huffed. "Small town. Gossip." She sighed. "Rumors run rampant in small-town Michigan."

A tiny sigh escaped Sabrina's mouth. "Do you think I should quit?"

Becki gave a short bark of laughter. "Not until you have another job or get called back to the pet food warehouse."

"I figured," she said. "My parents are pressuring me for money."

"Do you have any to spare?" Becki asked, adjusting her glasses.

"No." She needed to pay restitution and not her parents' unhealthy habits.

"You need to concentrate on finishing your parole and getting on with your life. I'm sure they'll manage," Becki said.

"I guess. I feel guilty I can't help them more."

Becki shook her head and tsk tsked. She picked up a paper on her desk and asked, "Have you been studying for your driver's test to get your license back?"

"No," Sabrina said again, intertwining her fingers together.

"That's the next step," Becki said, giving her a long look.

"The thought of driving scares me," Sabrina said.

"Understandable." Becki chewed her pen. "You should still prepare yourself." She pointed at her with the chewed pen. "Having a license will open up more opportunities for you."

Sabrina knew that, but her hands started to sweat when she thought about getting behind the wheel of a car—a car could kill the occupants or others on the road. How well she knew this.

Chapter 32

The next day, when Sabrina walked Maxi to school, there was a police officer by where Maxi and her classmates lined up before the bell sounded. Sabrina saw Olivia turn away and whisper something to the mother next to her. The group was mainly silent, but Sabrina heard a faint buzzing from several parents.

"Are you Sabrina Timmons?" The officer first looked at the group of parents and Olivia dipped her chin, before he turned to Sabrina.

What the heck?

Sabrina was the only one standing on the sidewalk; the other parents moved back and away little by little, but they watched, several straining forward to listen.

"Yes?" She studied the officer's face for signs he had made a mistake.

Had she done something wrong? *What did I do?* Her time in prison with the guards barking orders came hurtling back to her.

"We have a report that a sex offender is stalking the children."

Sabrina stepped back. "Do you mean me?"

"Yes," He looked at a tablet he held. "Are you Sabrina Timmons?"

"I am." Her voice shook and her heart did a crazy tap dance in her chest.

"Are you an ex-felon with orders to stay away from

children?"

"No. You have the wrong person." She lowered her voice to barely above a whisper. "True, I am an ex-felon." She felt her cheeks grow red, and several people walked by watching. "I went to prison for vehicular manslaughter. Five years."

He studied the tablet and his notes, then noticed Maxi. "Is that your child?"

Hmm. Yes but no? Technically no. "I'm her nanny."

"And who employs you, Miss Timmons?"

"Dr. Henry Comstock."

"Dr. Comstock." The officer looked confused. "I know him. Will you call him so I can speak to him?"

Sabrina pulled out her phone. "He doesn't always pick up depending on what's happening the E.R."

"Try, please. Maybe we can get this cleared up."

She called Henry's cell. It rang several times, but thankfully, Henry picked up.

"Henry? There's an officer here who'd like to speak with you."

"What's the problem?" He sounded alarmed.

"Just, a misunderstanding, I think."

"Sure, I'll talk to him." She heard the resignation in Henry's voice.

Was she causing him undue trouble?

Sabrina handed the phone to the officer.

"Dr. Comstock, Officer O'Casey here. Just checking on a report about a sex offender caring for your daughter."

Sabrina folded her arms and watched the officer's face turn from concern to surprise and then to acceptance.

"I'm sorry to have troubled you, sir. We have to check these things out. You may also get a visit from Child Protective Services." The officer was quiet. "We have to respond to these kinds of reports to keep the children of Clearwater safe. No..." The officer paused. "No, I can't tell you who made the report. Thank you for your time." He handed the phone to Sabrina.

Sabrina stared at the phone, but Henry had disconnected. She imagined Olivia called Social Services on her.

"I'm sorry to have delayed you, Miss Timmons," the officer said.

"I understand." She blew out her breath and rubbed her arms.

He dipped his chin and walked back to his black and white cruiser—the emblem of Clearwater on the sides—to serve and protect. Sabrina turned and spied Olivia by the corner of the building, watching. *Happy now?* Sabrina scowled.

She pushed her shoulders back, lifted her chin, and returned to Henry's house, willing the tears to wait until she was home.

When she entered the house, she felt the same disoriented swirl of emotions as the first time she had entered as Sabrina—the feeling of déjà vu.

Today, a buzzing filled her ears. Her mind went blank as she sank into the blue chair by the window—Alison's mother's favorite place to read. She needed comforting right now. But Henry was at work so there was no one.

Sabrina shook her head, but still, the buzzing stayed; the haziness of her mind cleared to form a picture of a man in a hospital bed with tubes snaking from his arms and nose—her father. Tears welled then and now for the man who looked like her father but yet wasn't. He was a kind man and loved her. He softly told her, "Come here, Alison, so I can see your lovely face."

"Oh, Daddy. Please don't go!"

He was her biggest champion. What would she do without him?

"I'm not sure the cancer will stop."

"I'm praying for it to go away," she said softly, taking his hand in hers—the same hand that had soothed her tears and bandaged scraped knees.

"It has a stronghold in my body."

Sabrina pushed herself from the blue chair and went to the bookcase to view the photo albums stored there. She pulled out one with a burgundy and gold cover and opened it. It was as if the past came pouring out.

Photos of her parents as teenagers before they wed. Pictures of them holding Alison, their only child. A picture of this very house as it was being built many years ago. Sabrina touched the pictures, wanting to take her parents' hands in hers again. It was worth relaying this love for Maxi no matter where her soul resided.

Her phone buzzed, breaking her concentration. She looked at the caller I.D.—her parents—who raised her.

"Hello?" she said hesitantly. It was never a good thing when they called.

"We're in a bind," her father explained. "We need some money to get a new place."

He explained they had gotten kicked out of her grandparents' house.

"I'm not sure I have much to give you."

"Anything!"

"I can send two hundred dollars."

She wrote down the address and would go to the bank and get a check to send. She found her voice. "I thought you were staying with Grandma and Grandpa."

"Not anymore. They've kicked us out. Something about taking their medications and draining their bank account."

That sounded so like Sabrina's parents.

"I don't have much money, and I got evicted from the apartment. I was laid off from my job, remember?"

Obviously, they hadn't remembered.

"You must have more money stashed somewhere?"

"I'm still paying restitution to the court."

"Can you skip a couple of payments?"

"No, I'll send the two hundred dollars."

"That won't go far."

"Are you and Mom working?"

"Sometimes."

Well, she guessed they needed to seek more permanent employment. She had her own problems here.

Chapter 33

As darkness fell and many people sat down to dinner, their doorbell rang. Henry, home from work, ushered in a woman from the social services department. She stood on the threshold, clutching a briefcase and wearing a grim frown.

The woman bustled in and handed Henry her card. "I'm checking on a report we took about a pedophile babysitting at this residence."

Henry shook his head. "There's a huge mistake. The woman I have babysitting isn't a pedophile."

The woman chewed her bottom lip, and her brows came together.

Henry drew Sabrina from the hallway where she stood watching.

"This is Sabrina, the babysitter."

"Are you on parole?"

"I am, but I'm not a pedophile."

The woman wrote something on the clipboard.

"What are you on parole for?"

"I caused an accident when I was in high school that killed a woman. I served almost five years."

"I see. Now you babysit for...?" The woman looked around.

"Maxi!" Henry called. "Can you come in here?"

Maxi did and stood next to Sabrina, pressing close to her. Sabrina put her arm around her. "What do you need, Daddy?"

"This lady wants to know who Sabrina babysits for."

"Are you Maxi?" The woman asked, and Maxi nodded. "Can I talk to you for a couple of minutes alone?" She looked at Henry. "Is that okay?"

Henry paused as if considering the request. "Yes, you can talk in here and we'll wait in the kitchen."

He led Sabrina away from the living room.

"I'm so sorry," she whispered when they entered the kitchen.

"No, I'm sorry. This is ridiculous! We can't have our lives being disrupted day in, day out! We'll move if we have to! Don't you worry—we all know this is bullshit!"

Sabrina swallowed. Henry was truly fired up. She didn't remember him ever being this upset. "This is all my fault."

"No." Henry shook his head. "Don't we all know whose fault this is and her name starts with O and ends with Livia…" He put his hands on Sabrina's shoulders, and she looked up at him. What was she seeing besides his pain-filled eyes?

"I'm…"

"No, we need you here." His fingers pressed into her shoulders.

Surely, her presence was causing more problems than help, though. Henry would likely get tired of all the disruptions in his life. And moving wasn't the answer. No one should move. He had wanted Maxi to grow up in this house. Maybe she should leave? But she couldn't with restitution hanging over her head. This was all Olivia's doing.

In prison, she had forgiven herself somewhat for the accident. Did she want hate in her heart about Olivia? Maybe Henry would find another woman to love him and Maxi—not Olivia, though—if she left.

"Dr. Comstock?" the woman from CPS called. It seems she wanted to talk to Henry as Maxi shuffled back to the kitchen.

Sabrina took Maxi's hand. "How was it, Pet?"

"It was okay. She asked me about inappropriate touching."

"What did you tell her?"

Maxi puffed out her chest. "I know about good and bad touches." Her brows knotted together. "Why is she mad at you?"

"I don't know." She was certain Olivia had turned Henry over to Child Protective Services to be spiteful and mean.

Henry came into the kitchen not a minute later and motioned with his chin. "She wants to talk to you now."

"Me?" Sabrina squeaked.

With growing dread, Sabrina walked down the hallway, dragging her feet to postpone the inevitable.

The woman, Gayle Swan, handed Sabrina her card. Sabrina sat with her hands in her lap and waited for the woman to question her.

"Tell me about your daily routine with Maxi?"

"Well, in the morning, I get her breakfast and help get her things together for school. Then I walk her to school." Sabrina felt her palms grow moist, and Gayle's business card was getting bent.

"In the evenings after school?"

"Homework, dinner, etc."

"How about bath time? Do you have to help wash

her?"

"No, she's almost eight and doesn't need my help."

"Aha, I see," she said, marking something down in her notebook. "How do you discipline Maxi?"

Sabrina gave a short, forced laugh. "I've never disciplined her! She's always so good."

Gayle quirked a brow like she didn't believe Sabrina's answer. "Tell me about your relationship with Dr. Comstock."

"We have a good relationship." Should she explain the walk-in soul idea? How would she? It would only make things worse for her, for them...

"You get along?" she prodded.

"Yes."

Gayle perused her list of questions, and once satisfied that she had asked the right ones, she turned off her tablet and thanked Sabrina for her time.

"What happens now?" Sabrina asked.

"Your case will be reviewed by a hearing panel, and we'll get in touch."

Sabrina sat looking at the door after Gayle left.

Henry joined her on the couch. "She left?" Henry asked, stating the obvious.

"Yes."

"You look a little pale," he said.

"I felt terrible about the questions she asked. Do people do those kinds of things to children?"

Henry ran his fingers through his hair. "Yes, yes, they do."

"I felt guilty, but I didn't do anything wrong."

He took her hand.

"Where's Maxi?" she asked.

"Homework. She wants to see you. I told her we

need to talk about grownup stuff," Henry said.

She turned to study him, trying to look into his thoughts at the moment. His face didn't give her any clues. "Is this over?" she asked in a tiny voice.

"I hope so."

She went to find Maxi. When Sabrina entered her bedroom, she could tell Maxi had been crying. "Why are you crying?"

"Is that mean woman going to take you away from me?"

"I hope not."

"Daddy says he'll fight it."

Sabrina nodded but rubbed her arms. No one had ever fought for her. How could she put Henry through this ordeal?

"Let's think of other things right now."

"Like what?" Maxi said with a sniff.

"How about we see what Wilber and Charlotte are up to?"

Maxi's face brightened as Sabrina picked up *Charlotte's Web* from the nightstand.

Later, Sabrina awoke to the squeak of her door and saw Maxi's figure in the doorway. "Can I sleep with you? I had a bad dream."

Would CPS question this sleeping arrangement? That assumption was ridiculous. Maxi was scared, and Sabrina moved over. Maxi got in and snuggled next to her, and Sabrina put an arm around her after smoothing down the quilt.

How could she leave this? Only when she heard Maxi's rhythmic and even breathing, did she drift off herself.

Henry looked confused when Maxi and Sabrina

emerged from her bedroom together in the morning. "Did you sleep with Sabrina last night?"

"I got scared." Maxi grabbed Sabrina's hand.

"Of what?"

"That woman asking questions about Sabrina."

Henry's gaze locked onto Sabrina's, and she gave him a small half shrug. He cleared his throat but didn't comment further.

Sabrina went into the bathroom to brush her teeth. She donned her robe and entered the kitchen to start the coffee.

"I'm sorry," she said as she poured coffee for him. "Would it be better if I went to see my parents in Detroit for a few weeks?"

"How could that possibly be better? Maxi and I need you," he said, putting down his phone and frowning at her.

"But you also need a consistent routine and not to be questioned about your choice of a nanny. Maxi's upset by the whole thing."

He nodded and grimaced. "She'd be more upset if you left."

She wasn't sure what she wanted to do.

Chapter 34

The following Thursday, she met her support group at the library. Most participants were sitting when she arrived. She noticed there was a new person, but when she got closer, her steps dragged. She knew that face.

Oh, God, why is he here?

He slumped down in his chair and narrowed his eyes at her. It had been a while, but he recognized her, and she him. She sat as far from him as she could.

"Welcome! We have a new participant today. Please welcome Daniel Hermanson," Chuck announced.

He was wearing baggy, ripped up jeans with a faded flannel, the sleeves pushed up, and a scowl on his pockmarked face. *Yup, the same ol' sleazy Danny,* she thought.

Danny's face still had hard edges and some new scars, but his eyes weren't red and darting. He must have gotten clean in prison.

He didn't acknowledge her, and she ignored him and automatically answered the questions asked. It was better not to make waves.

When they finished, Danny waited by the exit for her. "How ya doing?"

Sabrina rolled her eyes. *He had recognized me! I knew it!*

She steeled herself, preparing herself to talk to him.

She crossed her arms. "Oh, hey!" She tried to smile. "I'm okay, you?" She edged closer to the stairs to meet Maxi after school.

Danny shrugged. "When did you get out?" he asked.

"About eight months ago." She was close enough to see the scar that had bisected his lip.

"I just got out." He puffed out his chest. "Looking for a job."

"Try the pet food warehouse." Sabrina hoped that tip was friendly enough. They had called her back, but she declined because of her job caring for Maxi.

"I will. Thanks. You look good."

People pushed past them as they stood in the exit. Sabrina shuffled her feet—she wanted to go, too.

"Thanks." Sabrina tried smiling again. "I'm clean and got my GED and Associates."

"Wow! So, you're some big shot now, huh?" He nudged her side, and she genuinely smiled. "Wanna hang out?" Danny winked at her.

"Um," she stuttered. "I've got a babysitting job and need to get her from school." She felt panic rising and pushed it down. She had an hour to kill and didn't want to spend it with Danny from her past—a past she had left behind.

Danny didn't say anything and just blinked instead.

Sabrina shifted her feet. She felt extremely uncomfortable. With a deep breath, Sabrina told Danny no—she didn't want to hang out. To calm herself further, she thought of Maxi's sweet face.

His eyes narrowed. "You've turned into a real bitch, haven't you?"

And you're still the hard-assed Danny I remember.

She ignored him and hurried up the stairs far away from him and toward the elementary school. She didn't want to make the same mistakes as before. Besides, she had absolutely no feelings for Danny—not as a friend or as more.

When she was sure he hadn't followed her, she made a detour to the park and found a spot under the gazebo to read. She looked up to see a line of cars snaking past. Sabrina wasn't sure what had caught her attention, but something had. She stood, stretched, and watched the procession.

They turned into a gated area, which Sabrina had assumed was part of the park, but it wasn't—it was a cemetery, the Clearwater Cemetery. The park and the cemetery were neighbors separated by a spiked-iron fence covered with ivy and roses. She carefully put her book away and walked through the gates to see where the cars went.

There was a white canopy in the distance, where the people headed.

She had no wish to disturb them in their mourning. Instead of going right, she turned left to the section closest to the park. The tombstones were in neat rows; some had flowers or plants, and some were bare. Was Alison buried here?

The cemetery was quite large the farther she walked. Why hadn't she noticed it before? It was quiet and still, while the park was bustling with kids. She gravitated to the living and not the dead. But something had compelled her to explore further. She walked past names that had no meaning to her: Anderson, Smith, Johnson, and Williams. She slowed and stopped when she came to Larkin.

As she walked among the numerous Larkin graves, she recognized several. No, Sabrina didn't recognize the names. It was Alison who remembered and supplied faces for several of them. Dorothy Larkin—Rob's grandmother. She had met her once. Phillip Larkin—great-great-grandfather; the only knowledge of him was a black and white photo that graced Rob's mother's house. And then she came to Rob, and next to him—Alison Larkin Comstock.

She bent down to see the inscriptions and brushed away some dirt. There were fresh flowers on their adjoining graves. Had Henry done that?

She heard a car approach, stood, and dusted off her hands—Henry. She watched him exit his car and walk toward her in slow motion.

"Hi," he said with a wave. "Fancy meeting you here."

"I had never visited the cemetery before. I didn't even realize it was here," she said. As she talked, she moved her foot in the grass.

"A peaceful place, for sure."

"Alison's here?" She phrased it as a question, but it was more of a statement.

"Yes. She had bought plots when Rob died. I had her buried by him. But I also bought the plot next to her for me someday."

The thought brought tears to her eyes. She had no idea where the Timmonses were buried. Probably someplace in Detroit in pauper graves, she imagined.

Henry turned and pointed. "Alison's parents are buried over there."

"Do you come here often?"

"When I can. I know they are just bodies in the

ground. Their essences have found new bodies to love again."

"That sounds very romantic."

"I guess it is." He held his hand out to her. "Why don't we get Maxi from school together and go to the Moonglow for supper?" he suggested.

"I'd like that."

She took his hand, and they got in his car together and drove to Clearwater Elementary School.

Chapter 35

Today was Thursday, and she met with Becki, Chuck, and her support group. When she entered the library, she returned the books she had read. Her mind immediately went to checking out more books and the row of Clearwater High School yearbooks. *After*, she told herself. She'd study the books further after.

During the meeting, Danny turned slightly away and ignored her. *Fine with me*. She was glad. She had Henry on her mind, not Danny. She was a different person now, even though she looked the same. Her life had taken an unexpected U-turn, and she wanted nothing to do with Daniel Hermanson.

After group, she went to the library to browse the yearbooks. She sat on the floor, took out the three from their sophomore, junior, and senior years, and opened the first when a shadow fell over her—Danny.

"What do you want?" she asked, annoyed he had interrupted her time.

"Do you have any money?"

She looked up. His eyes reminded her of a wild animal—calculating and assessing his next meal—feral. Had she heard him correctly? "What?"

"I need some money." He shifted his feet as if he had an itch, and his hand twitched.

Is he using again?

"For the vending machines?" She thought it best to

play dumb.

He blew out a breath. "Something like that."

"I think I might have a dollar or two."

She reached into her front pocket until her fingers located a couple crumbled-up bills. "Here."

Danny squinted. "You don't have any more than that?" he asked. He took a step toward her. "You told me you were babysitting!" He snorted. "Babysitting my ass! I heard about the gig you have with the doctor." He smirked at her shocked face. "So, after you kill his wife, you shack up with him?"

She felt outraged by his words and could hardly spit out, "No." She struggled to stand up—being on the ground, with him looming over her, made her feel vulnerable. In fact, she wished someone from group or a librarian would come over. She gripped a yearbook to her chest as if it were a shield.

Danny grinned and let out a nasty laugh.

Danny's words were spiteful, but she had paid the ultimate price—prison. "I went to prison for five years!" she said incredulously.

"So I heard." He looked bored. His eyes darted around the room. He reached for her backpack. "I know you have more."

"Don't," she said, gritting her teeth, "touch my stuff." Sabrina snatched her bag back.

"I know you've got to have more than this." He opened his fist and looked at the bills and coins.

She didn't. "Are you using again?" Sabrina demanded. It seemed that way.

"Shut up!" Danny fiercely whispered, grabbing her arm. "Someone might hear you."

"Like Chuck?" She yanked her arm back. "You're

supposed to stay clean and sober. I want you to leave me alone!"

From nearby, someone cleared their throat. *Finally.* Sabrina let out a breath she didn't know she had been holding in. Danny frowned at the money clutched in his hand and threw it at her. "Keep your damn money!"

"Don't bother me again!" she said, feeling her cheeks flush with annoyance

Danny almost collided with a woman standing by the book-stacks as he hurried away.

"You okay?" the woman asked, frowning at Danny's retreating back. She bent down to collect the coins and bills on the floor. "Can I help you?" The woman handed the money to Sabrina, who returned it to her pack.

Sabrina gave her a tight smile. "I'm okay, it's okay. Thanks." Sabrina noticed her name badge. She was the assistant library director. Someone Sabrina hadn't met before.

Her galloping heart slowed, and she loosened her grip on the book she held.

"What are you doing?"

"Looking at old yearbooks," Sabrina said.

"Your parents?"

The question caused Sabrina to pause. *Honesty. Honesty and omission.* "Some people I once knew."

"Oh," the librarian said, backing away. "Let me know if I can be of help."

She opened the first yearbook with a blue cover and embossed metallic print: Clearwater High School Cavaliers. Sabrina began looking at the pictures as memories flashed like old-time movies through her mind.

Alison and Robert were prominent class members and involved in many activities. Alison looked very different from Sabrina with her curly light hair and delicate facial features—an elf or fairy. And Rob, too. He had the build of a football player, tall with broad shoulders. But he played baseball, Sabrina knew.

There was a picture of them together, and she studied their body language. They seemed to be leaning together as if they were one. They were a handsome couple, really—homecoming handsome. Rob's big muscular body dwarfed Alison's petite frame—opposites attract.

She and Henry were more alike than opposite. She guessed he was average at around six feet, with a lean runner's frame, and she was average height and weight—not petite in any way. They were more similar than different. Her head fit snugly under Henry's jaw like a puzzle piece the few times he had held her.

She turned the pages. One photo caused Sabrina to pause and study it further—Alison and the poetry club. One of Alison's poems, along with a group shot of stoic-looking students in black and white, was published on the page.

Our time at Clearwater High,
The catalyst for our future,
Good ol' Clearwater, we beseech thee,
Let us always remember these hallowed halls and the knowledge within,
Knowledge for all those who yearn it.

Sabrina frowned. The poem sounded like Alison—studious and serious in her pursuit to be an English teacher. Was Sabrina supposed to write poetry, too? She didn't think she could. No, she realized she could appreciate poetry and not write it herself.

Having Alison's soul made her like and enjoy many things she hadn't been exposed to before. She had never seen a book of poetry growing up at their apartment or a book for that fact, yet she loved to read and now enjoyed poetry. She had both street smarts and a love for the written words. Flipping through the yearbooks was like rereading a favorite novel; she knew the outcome but had forgotten some of the scenes.

She looked up at the clock. It was time to get Maxi from school, and she hadn't checked out any books. She'd peruse the bookshelves at Henry's for her next read. She carefully put the yearbooks back on the shelf to look at another time, shouldered her pack, and headed to the school, taking a shortcut between the library and the school complex—an alleyway filled with garbage bins and boxes.

By the dumpster, she first felt a sharp pain in her head and her vision went blurry. There was a throbbing throughout her body, then everything went numb and dark.

Chapter 36

Sabrina wasn't sure how long she had lain in darkness and pain; she opened her eyelid a fraction of an inch to a pinpoint of light and quickly closed it as nausea overtook her, and she vomited.

"She's here!" a voice yelled.

The sound was so close it made her wince and want to vomit again.

Sabrina wondered what "here" meant. Where was she? Had she been sleeping? Her head throbbed with the pulsing of blood, hammering her temples, and her mouth was thick and sour.

Hands touched her. Fingers pressed to her neck.

"I've got a pulse!"

Another hand checked her head.

Then, a familiar voice. "Oh, God, Sabrina!" She sensed Henry. He had her in his arms, in his lap. "Sabrina? Sabrina, can you hear me?"

Sabrina fluttered her eyelids and groaned. She smelled the spice of his hair gel as his fingers gently touched her head.

"Are you okay?" Henry asked, continuing to smooth her hair. "Can you tell me what happened?"

She could hear him—them, all of them, whoever they were—but the light hurt her eyes, and she squeezed them tight and managed to dip her chin in acknowledgment. Beyond the smallest gesture, her body responded with swirling and nausea.

"She's responding to me!" She heard Henry's voice explaining to the nearest person who would listen. "I'm Dr. Comstock," he said, his voice sounding pained. Then, more jumbled voices spoke as he replied, "I want her taken to…" Henry said then paused.

"Sabrina!" He cradled her in his arms. "We'll get you to the hospital! What happened? Tell me!" She felt his hand covering hers and a light squeeze. She tried to return the gesture, but her fingers felt sausage-like and numb.

She couldn't tell him what had happened—pain and black swirling clouds were all she recalled. But something was the matter.

Maxi! she remembered. *Where's Maxi?*

She didn't remember the ambulance ride or anything else until she opened her eyes tentatively in a seemingly bright room. In truth, the shades covering the windows were closed. The room wasn't bright, but leaving the blackness of her mind made her wince. Someone grasped her hand. Henry.

"You're awake," he whispered. He kissed her knuckles. "I was so worried." His finger traced down the faint blue veins on her arm that ended with a needle taped to her hand.

Her throat was raw, and she moved her fingers toward an enticing glass of water. "Water." The word was so soft she was afraid he wouldn't hear, but he did and put the straw to her lips.

"Easy."

The water flowed down her throat, soothing the rawness. Better. Henry took away the water. "You need to go slow, or you'll be sick again."

"Maxi?"

"She's with my mother."

She moved her head and cringed. "Wh…wha…what?"

"We don't know what happened for certain. The janitor found you in the alley." He gently pressed a cool, wet cloth to her head and wiped her face. "They're reviewing the security tapes from the school. The police think you were robbed. Your backpack is missing."

Danny. She was sure he had taken it from her. "Danny," she mumbled. "Dan…ny."

"Did you say, Danny?" He frowned. "The Danny from before?"

She moved her head slightly. Her eyes fluttered open and closed, taking in Henry and the hospital room. "Yes," she whispered. "He's out on parole and needed money."

His frown turned to anger, his eyes narrow and stormy, and his brows knitted. "Son of a bitch!" He clenched his fist. "I'll kill him!"

"You can't."

"Why not?"

"We need you." Pause. "Maxi and I." She managed a weak, feeble smile.

She heard a sob and a gasp, and then Henry put his head down and retook her hand. "I need you, too."

"I don't want you to go to prison," she said. "It's not a nice place."

He only gave her hand a slight squeeze.

They heard a knock on the door. "Hello?"

Sabrina felt Henry shift. She forced her eyes open and saw a shadowy figure in the doorway. Her eyes didn't seem to be cooperating, and she saw double.

"I'm Sergeant Brubaker. Are you Sabrina Timmons?"

"Yes." She pushed the remote on the bed to sit up as the officer approached her.

"I'm Dr. Comstock," Henry said, his hand slipping from hers and offering it to the officer.

"I've got a couple of questions. Can you help answer them?"

Sabrina moved her chin in acceptance. "I'll do my best."

"Do you know who hit you?"

"She thinks it might be Daniel, a drug dealer," Henry answered for her.

"Do you have his last name?"

H-E-R-M…then she remembered the rest of his name and said, "Hermanson."

"Is that who attacked you?" Officer Brubaker asked.

"I'm not sure, but Danny bothered me in the library about giving him money."

"Daniel Hermanson," the officer repeated the name, perhaps committing it to memory, but she also heard the rustle of paper. He may have written down the name too. After an eternity, he continued, "We're reviewing the surveillance tapes."

"I didn't see who hit me." Sabrina shook her head. "I just saw a shadow and then felt my head explode, and I must have passed out." She closed her eyes while gripping her head.

"Are you missing anything?" the officer asked.

She wasn't sure.

"Your backpack," Henry added.

"What was in there?" Officer Brubaker asked.

"Books, snacks, a notebook, library card, my phone, and a few dollars for the vending machine. Nothing of great value."

She kept her eyes closed, and her face felt flushed and warm. No doubt she had a fever of some kind. She moved her arm toward Henry. "I feel hot."

She felt him rise from his chair and heard the water running before he pressed a wet cloth to her forehead.

"Can we do this another time, officer?" Henry asked. "Clearly, she's had enough."

The officer cleared his throat. "We'll be in touch." He handed Henry his card and quietly left.

"Thank you," Sabrina whispered as he walked out, feebly waving an arm in farewell.

Hours later, she awoke to find Henry still by her side. "How are you feeling?" he asked, brushing her hair from her face.

She opened one eye and then the other. She wasn't seeing double, although her vision was still blurry. "I'm hungry." She saw Henry's face hovering over hers—a face lined with fatigue and worry.

"You're hungry?" He sounded joyous, like he just opened a Christmas present. "I'll get you some crackers and a pop."

"That sounds good."

Sabrina closed her eyes again and felt him leave, and the door softly closing behind him. Almost immediately, the door opened again. *Is Maxi here?* She peeked through her lashes. It wasn't Maxi, but the police officer from earlier. She forced her eyes open.

"I'm sorry to bother you again." He looked sheepish as he held out a tablet. "I have some pictures to share."

She nodded. "Come closer," she called. "My far vision is still blurry."

The ache in her temples had dulled like a receding headache, but her eyes were still adjusting.

He came to the side of the bed and showed her three pictures. One was a picture of someone holding what looked to be a tire iron raised over her head. The person wasn't very clear, but she saw his face.

"Do you recognize this man?"

It could be Danny or someone who closely resembled him. The officer swiped to a new photo. This next one was Danny's mug shot. Then, one from the library foyer showing Danny, his head tipped back, looking up at the camera.

"Yes."

The person brandishing the tire iron and the person in the library photo wore the same clothing—a black tee shirt with "Crank" embossed across the front.

"Is he Daniel Hermanson?"

"Yes." She swallowed.

"Do you know where we can find him?"

"No, sorry." She shook her head, but a pain stabbed her behind the eyes.

"What's your relationship with him?"

"We went to high school together." *And he was her drug dealer,* she added silently.

Her heart began to beat erratically. She pictured Maxi's sweet face and felt the tension leave her body. She finished answering the question.

"He's on parole and attends the same support group I do. At the library."

"Thank you for your time, Ms. Timmons. We'll be

in contact."

The door opened, and Henry returned.

"Doctor," the officer said with a nod.

"Do you have more information for us?" Henry juggled a can of soda and a few packages of crackers meant for soup.

"Ms. Timmons has identified Daniel Hermanson."

"Do you know where to find him?" Henry asked, putting the food down on the tray at the foot of her bed. Although Henry turned away from him, his words were tense and clear.

"We'll check with probation for an address."

"Good, I hope you lock him up."

"We do, too. Thank you."

Henry gave her a cracker when the officer left and some ginger ale. Her stomach settled from the soda bubbles, and she realized she hadn't eaten anything since lunch yesterday.

"Slowly," Henry advised. "You don't want it to come back up."

She nibbled on the cracker. It tasted so good she wanted to devour it, but she did as he requested.

"What kind of pictures did the officer show you?"

She sighed and opened her eyes to study the ceiling and light over the bed. "One from the library and alleyway and his mug shot."

"I hope they arrest him," Henry said, his voice low and menacing. "I'd like to hit him over the head and see what he feels like afterward!"

She suppressed a smile as she envisioned Henry brandishing a tire iron and smashing it down on Danny's head. Somehow, she couldn't see Henry mimicking Danny's actions. He was more apt to let the law handle people like Danny.

She hoped Danny was imprisoned again and she'd never have to see him or relive those memories.

The hospital released her the next day into Henry's care. His mother had been helping while she was in the hospital. When Henry guided Sabrina into the house, Beverly watched with arms crossed and suspicious eyes.

Henry put Sabrina to bed and closed the door, but Sabrina could hear snatches of their conversation.

"Is that who I think it is? Is she—is she—"

"I don't know, Mom." Henry interrupted. "Who do you think she is?"

"That...that girl...who." Beverly seemed to be having trouble spitting the words out.

Henry said, "She's Maxi's babysitter."

His voice was firm, and Beverly was quiet for the moment.

The truth was that Sabrina was tired from the hospital ordeal and didn't want to hear from Henry's mother. Her eyelids fluttered, and she closed and then opened them again. Beverly was just another reason Sabrina should leave.

Before she fell asleep, she heard, "How can she babysit in that condition?"

"She'll be well soon."

"Why are you paying her?" Beverly's voice ricocheted off Sabrina's tired and sore brain.

Sabrina pushed the blanket down and heard Henry make a loud noise with his throat.

"Are you sure she's a good influence on Maxi? What if Maxi decides on a life of crime because of this?"

"Gosh, Mom," Henry screeched. He sounded frustrated. "She won't. Sabrina was only seventeen when we had our accident."

"Accident?" his mother scoffed. "You mean *murder*!"

"Ssh, Mother! Sabrina's sleeping. I don't want you waking her up—and I don't need you making her upset!"

"Don't shush me! I care for Maxi and you. That woman's nothing but trouble!"

"We'll talk about this when Sabrina's well."

From far away, Sabrina heard the front door close.

Sabrina was causing Henry a whole lot of misery by being here. When she felt better, she'd leave and take the bus to Detroit and stay with her parents or grandparents. *Yes, that's what I'll do.*

No one seemed to like having her there except Henry and Maxi.

She wanted no more trouble for Henry. At that moment, she decided to leave as soon as she could. But oh, God, she'd miss them so much.

She could hardly think of not seeing them again. She squeezed her eyes shut, but the tears flowed. It would be the hardest thing she had ever had to do.

Chapter 37

Gradually Sabrina felt well enough to walk Maxi to school, and the lump on her head receded and Henry took out her stitches. Beverly went back to work, but Sabrina knew the woman disliked her and would be a thorn in her side.

Sabrina bit her lip at Henry's gentle touch and the way he smoothed back the strands from her face. Could she really leave him and Maxi? She had to; it was the only way she could see.

Beverly would always be a problem for Sabrina. It was just a matter of time when someone else threw another roadblock at them being together—another woman like Olivia. No, it would be for the best if she left. She imagined it would be hard for Henry and Maxi, but she was certain they would get on with their life without her.

With tears streaming down, she put underwear, jeans, and a shirt, the pictures and mementos from her childhood into her new backpack—the rest of her meager wardrobe she'd leave behind.

"You seem different, Sabrina," Maxi said when they returned after school.

"I do?" She frowned. "I guess I'm still recovering."

They had put twelve stitches on her scalp where the tire iron had bit into her head.

She needed to be more careful if Maxi could sense

she was getting ready to leave.

Sabrina also put a picture of Maxi and Henry in her pack so she could always remember them. She squeezed her eyes shut at the thought of never seeing them again.

The next afternoon with Maxi in school and Henry at work, Sabrina took her backpack, the money she had saved in a sock, and left by the side door. She wasn't sure where she was going, but she wouldn't stay here—her presence was upsetting to everyone.

What to do? She stood in the backyard, considering her options: stay or take the bus to Detroit…

The memories of barbecues in this backyard threatened to overturn her resolve. No, Maxi and Henry didn't need her memories. They needed someone they could count on. She was sure she'd have to return to Clearwater to testify at Danny's trial, but maybe she could stay at the women's shelter when she did.

She took out her phone and messaged Charlotte's mother and asked if Maxi could go home with them and Henry would pick her up later that evening.

That way, things could calm down with Henry's mother, and Sabrina could clear her head and evaluate her growing feelings toward Henry. But the thought of leaving Maxi made Sabrina's throat feel too small, and she swallowed repeatedly. Her feet turned toward the bus station and a trip to Detroit.

At the bus station, she bought a ticket and would message her parents she was coming. The bus didn't leave until four thirty. She'd have to wait two hours. She found a bench in the terminal and took out a book to read and also the picture of Maxi and Henry—their faces always calmed her. She was doing this for them, she told herself, but why did she feel like she was doing the wrong thing? Their faces turned wavy as she sniffed back her tears. She took out her phone and messaged her parents.

—*I'm coming for a visit.*—

Sabrina watched the blinking dots and could imagine her mother's face as she read those words.

—*Why?*—

Well, that wasn't the reply I expected!

—*I need to leave for a while.*— she typed.

—*Are you in trouble with the law?*—

—*No, something else.*— *Leave it to my parents to think it was something illegal I did...*she rolled her eyes.

—*Now isn't the best time.*—

Sabrina shifted in her seat as she waited for the bus. She still had over an hour before her departure.

—*I already have my ticket to Detroit*—

—*You should have let us know*—

—*I have some money for you*—

—*Why didn't you say so?!?*—

She knew that would get them. *Every time,* she thought. *Every. Time.*

—*The bus leaves soon*— she told them.

—*Let us know when you get here*—

She looked at the clock on the station wall—four p.m. Henry would be getting home soon and would discover her missing. She had left a note that Maxi was at a play date at Charlotte's. She could imagine his face—first surprise, then confusion, and then maybe he'd be mad.

****

When she heard the bus pull up by the door with a huff and squeal of the hydraulic brakes, Sabrina handed the driver her ticket and took a seat by the window. The sun had dimmed as they prepared to leave and it was as if a shroud had been pulled down outside her window seat.

Would Maxi run through the house calling for her?

She squeezed her eyes shut.

The rest of the passengers filed on, and the bus took off, lurching out of the parking lot and onto the street. She had almost five hours to figure something out. She needed to tell Becki she had left. What would this do to her parole? She hadn't thought about that aspect.

She heard the ping from her phone. Maybe her parents had better news?

It was from Henry.

—*Where are you?*—

—*I've left town.*— she typed. —*I guess living with you was a bad idea*—

—*Who said?*—

—*Your mother*—

—*Not to us. Not me. Not to Maxi*—

—*I don't want to cause problems*—

—*It's a problem not having you here. Maxi will be really upset when she gets home.*—

Her insides turned to mush at the thought of Maxi's tears.

—*Where are you?*—Henry asked. —*We'll talk*—

—*I'm on a bus headed to Detroit.*—

—*Shit*—

She stowed away her phone and turned to look out the window. Cars silently slipped past like eels in a river, gliding by the bus. The bus chugged along, but not at the same pace as the surrounding vehicles. After a while, she had lost track of time. One car seemed vaguely familiar, but she couldn't see who was driving. There must be a million four-door silver-gray sedans.

After about forty-five minutes, the bus took the exit to pick up more passengers in Grand Rapids. After they parked, Sabrina heard a scuffle and raised voices when the driver left the bus.

One voice sounded vaguely familiar. Henry's head popped up through the door, scanned the passengers, and hurried down the aisle to her seat.

"Sir! You can't get on without a ticket." Henry pushed around the driver.

"Sabrina." He grabbed her hands. "Please don't do this. Come back with me. We need you!"

"But I'm trouble." She hiccupped and tears threatened to overflow again.

He crouched down next to her seat.

"Are you proposing?" a woman from the back said, "I'll take pictures. This is so romantic!"

"I'm not proposing," Henry said, standing and smoothing his slacks. "My mother will calm down. She rarely likes anyone at first. Give her time. She didn't like Alison when she first met her."

"I remember," Sabrina said.

Henry grabbed both her hands. "You remember how that turned out?"

She nodded mutely.

"Then you know?" He pulled her up and into his arms. "She grew to love Alison."

She bobbed her head but kept her eyes down.

"Do you know what this means?" He lifted her chin.

"She'll eventually accept me?" Her tear-filled eyes locked onto Henry's.

"Yes."

"But Social Services and Olivia? That can't be good for your reputation."

"Screw my reputation. I want you, Alison, Sabrina, whoever!"

She smiled at the force of his words.

"Kiss her!" the woman in the back yelled, and someone whistled.

Henry bent over, and their lips met.

"Hey buddy," a guy in the next seat over said, "you can do better than that!"

Henry waved a hand while Sabrina laughed.

"I straightened it all out with Social Services, too," Henry whispered as Sabrina cupped his face and their gazes held. "Am I okay to kiss you again?"

"You better." Sabrina smiled. "Or there might be a riot from the other passengers."

He chuckled. "I don't care what they think. I only know I want you in our lives." He pulled her up against his chest.

This time, their lips locked in a passionate kiss, and her knees almost buckled. The other passengers clapped and cheered. She wanted him so much.

"Get a room!" someone joked from the back.

"We could," Henry pulled away. "That is, if you want?"

Sabrina tensed. "Where's Maxi?"

"Still at Charlotte's."

She surprised herself by saying, "Let's go home." *Her home*—the blue Craftsman house in Clearwater.

He looked down at her. "Do you mean it?"

She nodded mutely and whispered, "It might not ever be easy for us."

He added, "But we can handle anything as long as we're together."

Sabrina knew the other passengers were watching, and the bus driver was clearing his throat. She took her backpack, Henry wrapped his arms around her, and they exited the bus.

Once on the sidewalk, he turned to her again and gathered her in his arms. "Do you know what this means?" He didn't wait for an answer and buried his nose in her hair. "Rob and Alison can be together forever and ever, always," he whispered.

His arms were tight around her, and she couldn't see his face.

"What will people think of us together?"

"At this point, I don't give a damn what people think. They'll forget about us when the next bit of gossip comes their way." He paused to tuck a strand of hair behind her ear. "I want to be happy again, and I didn't have that until you came into my life and made my, I mean, *our* little girl happy."

"Forever and ever, always?" she whispered.

He squeezed her hand. "Yes."

She returned his squeeze.

A word about the author...

Sue writes award-winning speculative novels. The first book in this trilogy (Walk-Ins Welcome) won the Pencraft award for 'best chick lit.' She has been awarded 5-star reviews from Chanticleer, the Golden Wizard, and LitPick.

When Sue's not dreaming up unusual plots and characters or crafting chapters that keep readers up at night, she walks her dogs or attends Pilates classes. She loves to travel and see different nations and cultures, but she considers Nevada and Michigan her 'true homes' where she can recharge her batteries and see those she loves.

Thank you for purchasing
this publication of The Wild Rose Press, Inc.

For questions or more information
contact us at
info@thewildrosepress.com.

The Wild Rose Press, Inc.
www.thewildrosepress.com

www.ingramcontent.com/pod-product-compliance
Lightning Source LLC
Chambersburg PA
CBHW051646260626
47170CB00004B/1358